er filled the doorway, his eyes
...ering obsidian. But his voice
...cool with control. "I thought
...ere a team."

...swallowed. "I didn't know," she finally
...t.

...know what? Was there something
ambiguous about 'Don't tell anyone about this
...al'?"

"That was before it went through," she shot
...ck, refusing to give him another inch. But
...she really wanted, she finally admitted to
...erself, was him. Her boss. He was powerful
...charismatic, and he held her in his gaze in
a way no other man ever had.

The heat simmering between them was unbear-
able.

...m in the wrong. I can take it. What do you
...nt me to do?" She forced herself to ask
...m.

...ter actually smiled. There was a fire still
raging in his eyes, an unwavering desire. Her
mouth went dry. Un...

Barbara Dunlop writes romantic stories while [...] up in a log cabin in Canada's far north, where [...] outnumber people and it snows six months of the [...] Fortunately she has a brawny husband and two tee[...] children to haul firewood and clear the driveway [...] she sips cocoa and muses about her upcoming chapt[...] Barbara loves to hear from readers. You can contact he[...] through her website at www.barbaradunlop.com

BEAUTY AND
THE BILLIONAIRE

BY
BARBARA DUNLOP

MILLS & BOON®

All the characters in this book have no existence outside the imagination of the author, and have no relation whatsoever to anyone bearing the same name or names. They are not even distantly inspired by any individual known or unknown to the author, and all the incidents are pure invention.

First published in Great Britain 2009
Harlequin Mills & Boon Limited,
Eton House, 18-24 Paradise Road, Richmond, Surrey TW9 1SR

© Barbara Dunlop 2008

ISBN: 978 0 263 87452 5

Set in Times Roman 10½ on 12¾ pt
01-1109-41994

Harlequin Mills & Boon policy is to use papers that are natural, renewable and recyclable products and made from wood grown in sustainable forests. The logging and manufacturing process conform to the legal environmental regulations of the country of origin.

Printed and bound in Spain
by Litografia Rosés, S.A., Barcelona

BEAUTY AND THE BILLIONAIRE

For my editor, Kathryn Lye.
Who has the uncanny ability to track me down
anywhere in the world.

Prologue

A one-night stand only lasted one night. Sinclair Mahoney might be far from an expert, but she could guess that much.

So, while Hunter Osland's bare chest rose and fell in his king-size bed, and a door slammed somewhere in the far reaches of the mansion, she pushed her feet into her low-heeled black pumps and shrugged into her pinstriped blazer. She was only guessing at the protocol here, but she suspected it wasn't a lingering goodbye in the cold light of day.

Peacefully asleep in the gleaming four-poster, Hunter had obviously done this before. There were three brand-new toothbrushes in his en suite, along with half a dozen fresh towels and an assortment of mini toiletries in a basket on the marble counter. He had everything a woman needed if she wanted to make a simple, independent exit—which was exactly what Sinclair had in mind.

Last night had been good.

Okay, last night had been incredible. But last night was also over, and there was something pathetic about hanging around this morning hoping to see respect in his eyes.

So, she'd washed her face, brushed her teeth, and pulled her auburn hair into a simple ponytail, glancing one last time at the opulent cherry furnishings, the storm-tossed seascape that hung above his bed, and two potted palms that bracketed a huge bay window. It was nearly 8:00 a.m. She had just enough time to find her twin sister in the maze of the rambling Osland mansion. She'd say a quick goodbye before hopping a taxi to the Manchester, Vermont, airport and her flight to JFK.

She had a planning meeting at noon, then a conference call with the Cosmetics Manager at Bergdorf's. There were also two focus-group reports on Luscious Lavender beauty products tucked in her briefcase.

Last night was last night. It was time to return to her regular life. She squared her shoulders and reached for her purse, her gaze catching Hunter's tanned, toned leg. It had worked its way free from the tangled ivory sheets, and she followed its length to where the sheet was wrapped snugly around his hips.

She cringed at the telltale tightening beneath her ribs. His broad shoulders were also uncovered, along with the muscular arms that had held her tight into the wee hours of the morning. At five foot seven and a hundred and fifteen pounds, she wasn't used to feeling small and delicate in a man's arms. But she had in Hunter's.

In fact, she'd felt a lot of things she hadn't expected for a one-night stand.

Her friends had talked about them. But Sinclair had only imagined them. She always assumed they'd be stilted and awkward, each party self-conscious and trying to impress the other, while convincing themselves it wasn't tacky and shallow to sleep with a near stranger.

She'd been wrong about all of it.

There was an edge of the forbidden, sure. But Hunter had mostly been sweet and funny. At first, his intelligence had challenged her. Then his smile had enticed her. His touches and kisses had been the most natural things in the world. By the time they were naked, she felt as if she'd known him for years instead of hours.

In fact, standing here on the brink of goodbye, she could feel the heady sensations all over again. She wanted to turn back the clock, climb into the big, soft bed, taste those lips, run her fingertips over his skin, inhale the clean, woodsy scent of his hair.

She took a reflexive step forward.

But he shifted in the bed and she froze, appalled to realize she was about to hop in for round three. Or was it four? She supposed that depended on whether you counted his orgasms or hers.

He stretched his arm across the bed, and his expression drew taut in his sleep. He felt around and frowned.

Any second now, he would open his eyes. She knew somewhere deep down in her soul that if she was still standing here when he woke up, she'd be flat on her back in an instant. He knew his way past her defenses, knew a hundred ways to make her gasp and moan, knew all the right things to growl and whisper in her ear.

Her palm closed around her purse strap, and she commanded herself to back off.

He gave a bleary blink, and she grasped at the doorknob.

Before he could focus, she was out in the hall, shutting the door behind her and striding for the staircase.

It was over.
It was done.
Her best hope was to never see him again.

One

Hunter was here.

Six weeks later, Sinclair's stomach clenched around nothing as he strode into the Lush Beauty Products boardroom like he owned the place.

"—in a friendly takeover bid," Sinclair's boss, company president Roger Rawlings, was saying. "Osland International has purchased fifty-one percent of the Lush Beauty Products voting shares."

Sinclair reflexively straightened in her chair. Good grief, he *did* own the place.

Could this be a joke?

She glanced from side to side.

Would cameramen jump out any second and shove a microphone in her face? Were they filming even now to record her reaction?

She waited. But Hunter didn't even look her way, and nobody started laughing.

"As many of you are aware," said Roger, "among their other business interests, Osland International owns the Sierra Sanchez line of women's clothing stores across North America, with several outlets in Europe and Australia."

While Roger spoke, and the Lush Beauty managers absorbed the surprising news, Hunter's gaze moved methodically around the big, oval table. His gaze paused on Ethan from product development, then Colleen from marketing. He nodded at Sandra from accounting, and looked to Mary-Anne from distribution.

As her turn grew near, Sinclair composed her expression. In her role as public relations manager, she was used to behaving professionally under trying circumstances. And she'd do that now. If he could handle this, so could she. They were both adults, obviously. And she could behave as professionally as he could. Still, she had to wonder why he hadn't given her a heads-up.

The Hunter she'd met in Manchester had struck her as honorable. She would have thought he'd at least drop her an e-mail. Or had she totally misjudged him? Was he nothing more than a slick, polished player who forgot women the second they were out of his sight?

Maybe he didn't e-mail because he didn't care. Or, worse yet, maybe he didn't even remember.

In the wash of her uncertainty, Roger's voice droned on. "Sierra Sanchez will offer Lush Beauty Products a built-in, high-end retail outlet from which to launch the new Luscious Lavender line. We'll continue seeking other sales outlets, of course. But that is only one of the many ways this partnership will be productive for both parties."

Hunter's gaze hit Sinclair.

He froze for a split second. Then his nostrils flared, and his eyebrows shot up. She could swear a current cracked audibly between them. It blanketed her skin, shimmied down her nervous system, then pooled to a steady hum in the pit of her stomach.

Hunter's jaw tightened around his own obvious shock.

Okay. So maybe there was a reason he hadn't given her a heads-up.

There were days when Hunter Osland hated his grandfather's warped sense of humor. And today ranked right up there.

In the instant he saw Sinclair, the last six weeks suddenly made sense—Cleveland's insistence they buy Lush Beauty Products, his demand that Hunter take over as CEO, and his rush to get Hunter in front of the company managers. Cleveland had known she worked here, and he'd somehow figured out Hunter had slept with her.

Hunter's grandfather was, quite literally, forcing him to face the consequences of his actions.

"So please join me in welcoming Mr. Osland to Lush Beauty Products," Roger finished to a polite round of applause. The managers seemed wary, as anyone would be when the corporate leadership suddenly shifted above them.

It was Hunter's job to reassure them. And he now had the additional duty of explaining himself to Sinclair. God only knew what she was thinking. But, talking to her would have to wait. He refocused his gaze on the room in general and moved to the head of the table.

"Thank you very much," he began, smoothly taking control of the meeting, like he'd done at a thousand meetings before. "First, you should all feel free to call me Hunter. Second, I'd like to assure you up front that Osland International has no plans to make staffing changes, nor to change the current direction of Lush Beauty Products."

He'd mentally rehearsed this next part, although he now knew it was a lie. "My grandfather made the decision to invest in this company because he was excited about your product redevelopment—such as the Luscious Lavender line—and about your plans to expand the company's target demographic."

Hunter now doubted Cleveland had even heard of Lush Beauty Products before meeting Sinclair. And Cleveland would be a lot less excited about the product redevelopment than he was about yanking Hunter's chain.

"Osland International has analyzed your success within the North American midprice market," Hunter told the group. "And we believe there are a number of opportunities to go upscale and international. We're open to your ideas. And, although Roger will continue to manage day-to-day operations, I'll be hands-on with strategic direction. So I want to invite each of you to stop by and see me. I expect to be on site several days a month, and I believe I'll have an office on the twentieth floor?"

He looked to Roger for confirmation.

"Yes," said Roger. "But if any of you have questions or concerns, you should feel free to use me as a sounding board."

The words surprised Hunter. Was Roger telling them not to go directly to Hunter?

"We'll try to make this transition as smooth as possible," Roger continued in a silky voice that set Hunter's teeth on edge. "But we understand some of you may feel challenged and unsettled."

Oh, great little pep talk. Thanks for that, Roger.

"There's no need for anyone to feel unsettled," Hunter cut

in. "As far as I'm concerned, it's business as usual. And my door is always open." Then he looked directly at Sinclair. "Come and see me."

An hour later, Sinclair took Hunter up on his invitation. On the twentieth floor, she propped herself against the doorjamb of his airy corner office. "This," she said, taking in the big desk, the credenza piled with books and the meeting table that sat eight, "I have *got* to hear."

He straightened in his high-backed chair and glanced up from his laptop, a flash of guilt in his eyes.

Ignoring the way her heart lifted at his reaction, she took two steps inside and closed the door behind her. He cared that he'd blindsided her. At least that was something.

Not that she cared about him in any fundamental way. She couldn't. They were a brief flash of history, and nothing more.

"It was Gramps," answered Hunter. "He bought the company and sent me here to run it."

"And you didn't know about me?" she guessed.

"I didn't know," he confirmed.

"So, you're not stalking me?"

He hit a key on his computer. "Right. Like any reasonable stalker, I bought your company to get close to you."

She shrugged. "Could happen."

"Well, it didn't. This is Gramps' idea of a joke. I think he knows I slept with you," said Hunter.

"Then there's something wrong with that man." And there was something frightening about a person with enough economic power to buy a four-hundred-person company as a joke. There was something even more frightening about a person who took the trouble to actually do it.

"I think he's losing it in his old age." Then Hunter paused

for a moment to consider. "On the other hand, he was always crotchety and controlling."

"Kristy likes him," said Sinclair. Not that she was coming down on Cleveland Osland's side. If Hunter was right, the man was seriously nuts.

"That's because he's batty over your sister."

Sinclair supposed that was probably true. It was Cleveland Osland who had helped Kristy get started in the fashion business last month. And now her career was soaring.

A soaring career was what Sinclair wanted for herself. And what she really wanted was for Hunter not to be a complication in that. She had a huge opportunity here with the planned company expansion and with the development of the new Luscious Lavender line.

She advanced on his wide desk to make her point, forcing herself to ignore the persistent sexual tug that had settled in her abdomen. Whatever they'd had for that brief moment had ended. He was her past, now her boss.

Even if he might be willing to rekindle. And she had no reason to assume he was willing. She was not.

She dropped into one of his guest chairs, keeping her tone light and unconcerned. "So what do we do now?"

A wolfish grin grew on his face.

All right, so maybe there was a reason to assume he was willing.

"No," she said, in a stern voice.

"I didn't say a word."

"You thought it. And the answer is no."

"You're a cold woman."

"I'm an intelligent woman. I'm not about to sleep my way to the top."

"There's a lot to be said for being at the top."

"I guess you would know."

He leaned back in his chair, expression turning mischievous. "Yeah. I guess I would."

She ignored the little-boy charm and leaned forward to prop her elbows on his desk. "Okay, let's talk about how this works."

"I thought we'd pretty much demonstrated how it worked last month."

She wished he'd stop flirting. It was ridiculously tempting to engage. Their verbal foreplay that night had been almost as exciting as the physical stuff.

"Nobody here knows about us," she began, keeping her tone even.

"I know about us," he pointed out.

"But you're going to forget it."

"Not likely," he scoffed.

She leaned farther forward, getting up into his face. "Listen carefully, Hunter. For the purposes of our professional relationship, you are going to forget that you've seen me naked."

"You know, you're very cute when you're angry."

"That's the lamest line I've ever heard."

"No, it's not."

"Can you be serious for a second?"

"What makes you think I'm not serious?"

"Hunter."

"Lighten up, Sinclair."

Lighten up? That was his answer?

But she drew back to think about it. Could it be that simple? "Am I making too much of this?"

He shrugged. "I'm not about to announce anything in the company newsletter. So, unless you spread the word around the water cooler, I think we're good."

She eyed him up. "That's it? Business as usual?"

"Gramps may have bought Lush Beauty Products for his own bizarre reasons. But I'm here to run it, nothing more, nothing less. And you have a job to do."

She came to her feet and gave a sharp nod, telling herself she was relieved, not disappointed, that it would be easy for him to ignore their past.

"See you around the water cooler, I guess," she said in parting.

"Sure," Hunter responded. "Whatever."

Despite the casual goodbye, Hunter knew it would be hell trying to dismiss what they'd shared. As the office door closed behind her, he squeezed his eyes shut and raked a hand through his hair. Their past might have been short, but it was about as memorable as a past could get.

For the thousandth time, he saw Sinclair in the Manchester mansion. She was curled in a leather armchair, beneath the Christmas tree, next to the crackling fireplace. He remembered thinking in that moment that she was about as beautiful as a woman could get. He'd always had a thing for redheads.

When he was sixteen years old, some insane old gypsy had predicted he'd marry a redhead. Hunter wasn't sure if it was the power of suggestion or a lucky guess, but redheads were definitely his dates of choice.

The flames from the fire had reflected around Sinclair, highlighting her rosy cheeks and her bright blue eyes. Her shoulder-length hair flowed in soft waves, teasing and tantalizing him. He'd already discovered she was smart and classy, with a sharp wit that made him want to spar with her for hours on end.

So he'd bided his time. Waiting for the rest of the family to head for bed, hoping against hope that she'd stay up late.

She had.

And then they were alone. And he had been about to make a move. She was his cousin's new sister-in-law, and he knew their paths might cross again at some point. But he couldn't bring himself to worry about the future. There was something intense brewing, and he owed it to both of them to find out what it was.

He came to his feet, watching her closely as he crossed the great room. Her blue eyes went from laughing sapphires to an intense ocean storm and, before he even reached her chair, he knew she was with him.

He stopped in front of her, bracing a hand on either arm of the chair, leaning over to trap her in place. She didn't flinch but watched him with open interest.

He liked that.

Hell, he loved that.

"Hey," he rasped, a wealth of meaning in his tone and posture.

"Hey," she responded, voice husky, pupils dilated.

He touched his index finger to her chin, tipping it up ever so slightly.

She didn't pull away, so he bent his head, forcing himself to go slow, giving her plenty of time to shut him down. He could smell her skin, feel the heat of her breath, taste the sweet explosion of her lips under his.

His free hand curled to a fist as he steeled himself to keep the kiss gentle. He fought an almost overwhelming urge to open wide, to meet her tongue, to let the passion roar to life between them.

Instead, he drew back, though he was almost shaking with the effort.

"Stop?" he rasped, needing a definite answer, and needing it *right now*.

"Go," she replied, and his world pitched sideways.

With a groan of surrender, he dropped to one knee, clamping a hand behind her neck, firmly pulling her forward for a real kiss.

There was no hesitation this time. Their tongues met in a clash. She shifted in the chair to mold against him, her breasts plastered against his chest while desire raced like wildfire along his limbs.

Her hair was soft, her breath softer, and her body was pure heaven in his arms.

"I want you," he'd muttered.

"No kidding," she came back.

His chuckle rumbled against her lips. "Sassy."

"You know it," she whispered in the instant before he kissed her all over again.

The kiss went harder and deeper, until he finally had to gasp for air. "Can I take that as a yes?"

"Can I take that as an offer?" she countered.

"You can take it as a promise," he said, and scooped her into his arms.

She placed her hands on his shoulders and burrowed into the crook at his neck. Then her teeth came down gently on his earlobe. Lust shot through him, and he cursed the fact that his bedroom was in a far corner on the third floor.

A knock on his office door snapped him back to reality.

"Yeah?" he barked.

The door cracked open.

It was Sinclair again.

She slipped inside, still stunningly beautiful in that sleek ivory skirt and the matching blazer. Her pale-pink tank top molded to her breasts, and her shapely legs made him long to trail his fingertips up past her hemline.

"Since it's business as usual," she began, perkily, crossing the room, oblivious to his state of discomfort.

"Right," he agreed from between clenched teeth.

"I have something I'd like to discuss with you."

At the moment, he had something he wished he could discuss with her, too.

"Fire away," he said instead.

She took up the guest chair again and crossed her legs. Her makeup was minimal, but she didn't need it. She had a healthy peaches-and-cream glow, accented by the brightest blue eyes he'd ever seen. Sunlight from the floor-to-ceiling bay window sparkled on her hair. It reminded him of the firelight, and he curled his hands into new fists.

"I have this idea."

He ordered himself to leave that opening alone.

"Roger's been reluctant to support it," she continued.

She wanted Hunter to intervene?

Sure. Easy. No problem.

"Let's hear it," he said.

"It's about the ball."

Hunter had just read about the Lush Beauty Products' Valentine's Ball. They were going to use it to launch the Luscious Lavender line. It was a decent idea as publicity went. Women loved Valentine's Day, and the Luscious Lavender line was all about glamming up and looking your best.

"Shoot," he told her.

"I've taken the lead in planning the ball," she explained, wriggling forward, drawing his attention to the pale tank top. "And I've been thinking we should go with something bigger."

"A bigger ball?" He dragged his attention back to her face. They'd rented the ballroom at the Roosevelt Hotel. It didn't get much bigger than that.

Sinclair shook her head. "Not a bigger ball. A bigger product launch. Something more than a ball. The ball is fine.

It's great. But it's not…" Her lips compressed and her eyes squinted down. "Enough."

"Tell me what you had in mind," he prompted, curious about how she conducted business. He'd been struck by her intelligence in Manchester. It would be interesting to deal with her in a new forum.

"What I was thinking…" She paused as if gathering her thoughts. "Is to launch Luscious Lavender at a luxury spa. In addition to the ball." Her voice sped up with her enthusiasm. "We're going after the high-end market. And where do rich women get their hair done? Where do they get their facials? Their body wraps? Their waxing?"

"At the spa?" asked Hunter, trying very, very hard not to think about Sinclair and waxing.

She sat back, pointed a finger in his direction, a flush of excitement on her face. "Exactly."

"That's not bad," he admitted. It was a very good idea. He liked that it was unique, and it would probably prove effective. "What's Roger's objection?"

"He didn't tell me his objection. He just said no."

"Really?" Hunter didn't care for autocracy and secrecy as managerial styles. "What would you like me to do?"

Whatever it was, he'd do it in a heartbeat. And not because of their history. He'd do it because it was a good idea, and he appreciated her intelligence and creativity. Roger better have a damn good reason for turning her down.

"If you can clear it with Roger—"

"Oh, I can clear it with Roger."

Her teeth came down on her bottom lip, and a hesitation flashed through her eyes. "You agreed awfully fast."

"I'm agile and decisive. Got a problem with that?"

"As long as…" Guilt flashed in her eyes.

"I'm reacting to your idea, Sinclair. Not to your body."

"You sure?"

"Of course, I'm sure." He was. Definitely.

"I was going to approach New York Millennium." She named a popular spa in the heart of Manhattan.

"That sounds like a good bet. You need anything else?"

She shook her head, rising to her feet. "Roger was my only roadblock."

Jan Colley

Two

"Obviously," Roger said to Sinclair, with exaggerated patience. "I can't turn down the CEO."

She nodded where she sat in a guest chair in his office, squelching the lingering guilt that she might have used her relationship with Hunter as leverage. She admitted she'd been counting on Roger having to say yes to Hunter.

But she consoled herself in being absolutely positive the spa launch was a worthwhile idea. Also, Roger had been strangely contrary lately, shooting down her recommendations left and right. It was all but impossible to do her job the way he'd been micromanaging her. Going to Hunter had been her option of last resort.

Besides, Hunter had invited all the employees to run ideas past him. She wasn't taking any special privilege.

"I'm not holding out a lot of hope of you securing the Millennium," warned Roger.

Sinclair was more optimistic. "It would be good for them, too. They'd have the advantage of all our advance publicity."

Roger came to his feet. "I'd like you to take Chantal with you."

Sinclair blinked as she stood. "What?"

"I'd appreciate her perspective."

"On…" Sinclair searched for the logic in the request.

Chantal was a junior marketing assistant. In her two years with the company, she'd mostly been involved in administrative work such as ad placement and monitoring the free-sample program.

"She has a good eye," said Roger, walking Sinclair toward the door.

A good eye for what?

"And I'd like her to broaden her experience," he finished.

It was on the tip of Sinclair's tongue to argue, but she had her yes, so it was time for a strategic retreat. She'd figure out the Chantal angle on her own.

Her first thought was that Roger might be grooming the woman for a public relations position. Sinclair had been lobbying to get an additional PR officer in her department for months now, but she had her own assistant, Amber, in mind for the promotion, and Keely in reception in mind for Amber's job.

"Keep me informed," insisted Roger.

"Sure," said Sinclair, leaving his office to cross the executive lobby. First she'd set up a meeting at the Millennium, then she'd sleuth around about Chantal.

Three days later, Sinclair lost the Millennium Spa as a possibility. The President liked Lush's new samples, but he claimed using them over the launch weekend would put him in a conflict with his regular beauty products supplier.

She'd been hoping the spa would switch to Luscious

Lavender items on a permanent basis following the launch. But when she mentioned that to the spa President, he laughed and all but patted her on the head over her naiveté. Supply contracts, he told her, didn't work that way.

Chantal had shot Sinclair a smug look and joined in the laughter, earning a benevolent smile from the man along with Sinclair's irritation.

Then the next day, at a pre-Valentine's event at Bergdorf's on Fifth Avenue, Chantal earned Sinclair's irritation all over again.

It was twelve days before Valentine's Day and the main ball and product launch. Sinclair had worked for months preparing for both events.

For Bergdorf's, she'd secured special space in the cosmetics department, hired top-line professional beauticians, and had placed ads in *Cosmopolitan, Elle* and *Glamour.* She'd even talked Roger into an electronic billboard in Times Square promoting the event. Her spa plan might have fallen flat, but she knew if they could get the right clientele into Bergdorf's today for free samples and makeovers, word of mouth would begin to spread in advance of the ball.

The event should have come off without a hitch.

But at the last minute Roger had inserted Chantal into the mix, displacing one of the beauticians and making the lineups unnecessarily long. Amber, who had already heard about Chantal's appearance at the spa meeting, was obviously upset by this latest turn of events. Sinclair didn't need her loyal employee feeling uncertain about her future.

The result had been a long day. And as the clock wound toward closing time, Sinclair was losing energy. She did her hourly inventory of the seven makeover stations, noting any dwindling supplies on her clipboard. Then she handed the list to Amber, who had the key to the stockroom and was in charge of replenishing.

She reminded the caterers to do another pass along the lineup, offering complimentary champagne and canapés to those customers who were still waiting. The cash register lineup concerned her, so she called the store manager on her cell, asking about opening another till.

The mirrors on stations three and six needed a polish, so she signaled a cleaner. In the meantime, she learned they were almost out of number five brushes and made a quick call to Amber in the back.

"How's it going?" Hunter's voice rumbled from behind her.

She couldn't help but smile at the sound, even as she reflexively tamped down a little rush of pleasure. They hadn't spoken in a few days and, whether she wanted to or not, she'd missed him. She twisted to face him, meeting his eyes and feeling her energy return.

"Controlled chaos," she mouthed.

"At least it's controlled." He moved in beside her.

"How are things up on the executive floor?" she asked.

"Interesting. Ethan gave me a tour of the factory," Hunter made a show of sniffing the back of his hand. "I think I still smell like a girl."

"Lavender's a lovely scent," said Sinclair, wrinkling her nose in his direction. She didn't detect lavender, just Hunter, and it was strangely familiar.

"I prefer spice or musk."

"Is your masculinity at stake?"

"I may have to pump some iron later just to even things up."

"Are you a body builder?"

Even under a suit, Hunter was clearly fit.

"A few free weights," he answered. "You?"

"Uh, no. I'm more of a yoga girl."

"Yoga's good."

"Keeps me limber."

"Okay, not touching that one."

"You're incorrigible."

"My grandfather would agree with you on that point."

A new cashier arrived, opening up the other till, and the lineup split into two. Sinclair breathed a sigh of relief. One problem handled.

Then she heard Chantal's laughter above the din and glanced at the tall blonde, who wore a cotton-candy-pink poof-skirted minidress and a pair of four-inch gold heels. She was laughing with some of the customers, her bright lips and impossibly thick eyelashes giving her the air of a glamorous movie star.

With Hunter here, Sinclair felt an unexpected pang of self-consciousness at the contrast between her and Chantal. Quickly, though, she reminded herself that her two-piece taupe suit and matching pumps were appropriate and professional. She also reminded herself that she'd never aspired to be a squealing, air-kissing bombshell.

She tucked her straight, sensibly cut hair behind her ears.

"So what happened at the spa?" asked Hunter.

"Unfortunately, it was a no go."

"Really?" He frowned with concern. "What was the problem?"

"Some kind of conflict with their supplier."

"Did you—"

"Sorry. Can you hang on?" she asked him, noticing a disagreement brewing between the new cashier and a customer. She quickly left Hunter and moved to step in.

It turned out the customer had been quoted a wrong price

by her beautician. Sinclair quickly honored the quote and threw in an extra tube of lipstick.

When she looked back, Chantal had crossed the floor. She was laughing with Hunter, a long-fingered, sparkly-tipped hand lightly touching his shoulder for emphasis about something.

He didn't seem the least bit disturbed by the touch, and an unwelcome spike of annoyance hit Sinclair. It wasn't jealousy, she quickly assured herself. It was the fact that Chantal was ignoring the customers to flirt with the CEO.

Sinclair made her way along the counter.

"Chantal," she greeted, putting a note of censure in her voice and her expression.

"I was just talking to Hunter about the new mousse," Chantal trilled. Then she fluffed her hair. "It works miracles."

Sinclair compressed her lips.

In response, Chantal's gaze took in Sinclair's plain hairstyle. "You should…" She frowned. "Uh…have you *tried* it?"

Hunter inclined his head toward Sinclair. He seemed to be waiting for her answer.

"No," Sinclair admitted. She hadn't tried the new mousse. Like she had time for the Luscious Lavender treatment every morning. She started work at seven-thirty after a streamlined regime that rarely included a hairdryer.

"Oh." Chantal pouted prettily.

Sinclair nodded to a pair of customers lingering around Chantal's sample station. "I believe those two ladies need some help."

Chantal giggled and moved away.

"Nice," said Hunter after she left.

"That better have been sarcasm."

All men considered Chantal beautiful, but Sinclair would

have been disappointed in Hunter if he hadn't been able to see past her looks.

"Of course it was sarcasm." But his eyes lingered on the woman.

Sinclair elbowed him in the ribs.

"What?"

"I can tell what you're thinking."

"No, you can't."

"Yes, I can."

"What am I thinking?"

"That her breasts are large, her skirt is short, and her legs go all the way to the ground."

Hunter coughed out a laugh.

"See?" blurted Sinclair in triumph.

"You're out of your mind."

"The doors are closing," murmured Sinclair, more to herself than to Hunter, as she noticed the security guards stop incoming customers and open the doors for those who were exiting.

"You got a few minutes to talk?" he asked.

"Sure." Hunter was the CEO. She was ready to talk business at his convenience.

She nodded to two empty chairs across the room.

They moved to the quiet corner of the department, and Sinclair climbed into one of the high leather swivel chairs. She parked her clipboard on the glass counter.

Hunter eased up beside her. "So what's the plan now?"

She glanced around the big room. "The cleaning staff will be here at six. Amber will make sure the leftover samples are returned to the warehouse. And I'll write a report in the morning." Later tonight, she was going to start painting her new apartment, but she didn't think Hunter needed that kind of information.

His gray eyes sparkled with merriment. "I meant your plan about the spa."

"Oh, that." She waved a hand. "It's dead. We couldn't make a deal with the Millennium."

Her gaze unexpectedly caught Chantal. The woman was eyeing them up from across the room, tossing her glittering mane over one shoulder and licking her red lips.

Under the guise of more easily conversing, Sinclair scooted a little closer to Hunter. Let miss Barbie-doll chew on that.

Hunter slanted a look toward Chantal, then shot Sinclair a knowing grin.

"Shut up," she warned in an undertone.

"I never said a word."

"You were thinking it."

"Yeah. And I was right, too."

Yeah, he was. "It's something Pavlovian," she offered.

His grin widened.

"I didn't want her to think Luscious Lavender mousse trumps brains, that's all."

"It doesn't."

"I don't even use mousse. It's nothing against Luscious Lavender. It's a personal choice."

"Okay," said Hunter.

"Kristy has always been the glitter and glam twin. I'm—"

"Don't you dare say plain Jane."

"I was going to say professional Jane."

He snorted. "You don't need a label. And you shouldn't use Kristy as a frame of reference."

"What? You don't compare yourself to Jack?"

"I don't." But his expression revealed a sense of discomfort.

"What?" she prompted.

"Gramps does."

Sinclair could well imagine. "And who comes out on top?"

Hunter raised an eyebrow. "Who do you think?"

"I don't know," she replied honestly. Jack seemed like a great guy. But then so did Hunter. They were both smart, handsome, capable and hard-working.

"Jack's dependable," said Hunter. "He's patient and methodical. He doesn't make mistakes."

Sinclair found herself leaning even closer, the noise of the store dimming around them as the last of the customers made their way out the door. "And you are?"

"Reckless and impulsive."

"Why do I hear Cleveland's voice when you say that?"

Hunter chuckled. "It's usually accompanied by a cuff upside the head."

In the silence that followed, Sinclair resisted an urge to take his hand. "That's sad," she told him.

"That's Gramps. He's a hard-ass from way back." Then Hunter did a double take of her staring. "Don't look at me like that."

She swallowed. "I'm sorry."

"It makes me want to kiss you," he muttered.

"Don't you—"

"I'm not going to kiss you." He glanced back to Chantal. "*That* would definitely make the company newsletter." He focused on Sinclair again. "But you can't stop me from wanting to."

And she couldn't stop herself from wanting to kiss him back. And it didn't seem to matter what she did to try and get rid of the urge, it just grew worse.

"What can we do about this?" She was honestly looking for help. If the feelings didn't disappear, they were going to trip up sooner or later.

Hunter rose to his feet.

"For now, I'm walking out the door. Chantal is already wondering what we're talking about."

Sinclair shook herself and rose with him. "Check." If they weren't together, they couldn't give in to anything.

"But later, I need to talk to you."

She opened her mouth to protest. Later didn't sound like a smart move to her at all.

"About the spa," he clarified. "Business. I promise. What are you doing tonight?"

"Painting my apartment."

"Really?" He drew back. "That's what you do on Saturday night?"

Yeah, that was what she did on Saturday night. She rattled on, trying not to seem pathetic. "I just bought the place. A great little loft in Soho. But the colors are dark and the floor needs stripping, and the mortgage is so high I can't afford to pay someone to do it for me."

"You want a raise?"

"I want a guy with sandpaper and a paint roller."

"You got it."

"Hunter ——"

"Give me your address. We can talk while we paint."

Her and Hunter alone in her apartment? "I don't think—"

"I'll be wearing a smock and a paper cap. Trust me, you'll be able to keep your hands off."

"Nothing wrong with your ego."

He grunted. "I know you can't resist me under normal circumstances."

"Ha!" The gauntlet thrown down, she'd resist him or die trying.

Now that she thought about it, maybe painting together

wasn't such a bad idea. Hunter's family had bought the company. He was a permanent part of Lush Beauty Products, and the sooner they got over this inconvenient hump, the better. In fact, it was probably easier if they smoothed out the rough spots away from Chantal's and other people's prying eyes.

"Seventy-seven Mercy Street," she told him with a nod. "Suite 702."

"I'll be there."

On his way to Sinclair's house, Hunter stopped in at the office. He was pretty sure Ethan Sloan would still be around. By all accounts, Ethan was a workaholic and a genius. He'd been with Lush Beauty Products for fifteen years, practically since the doors opened with a staff of twenty and a single store.

He had developed perfumes, hair products, skin products and makeup. The man had a knack for anticipating trends, moving from floral to fruit to organic. In his late thirties now, he'd wisely set his sights on fine quality, recognizing a growing segment of the population with a high disposable income and a penchant for self-indulgence.

Hunter was also willing to bet Ethan had a knack for management and the underlying politics of the company. And Hunter had some questions about that.

He found Ethan in his office, on the phone, but the man quickly motioned to Hunter to sit down.

"By Thursday?" Ethan was saying as Hunter took a seat and slipped open the button on his suit jacket.

Ethan was neatly trimmed. Hunter had noticed that he generally wore his shirtsleeves rolled up, although he'd wear a jacket on the executive floor. Smart man.

"Great," said Ethan, nodding. "Sign 'em up. Talk to you then."

He hung up the phone. "New supplier for lavender," he explained to Hunter. "Out of British Columbia."

"We're running short?"

"Critically. And it's our key ingredient." He rubbed his hands together. "But it's solved now. What can I do for you?"

Hunter settled back in his chair. "Not to put you on the spot. And way off the record."

Ethan smiled. He brought his palms down on the desktop, standing to walk around its end and close the office door. "Gotta say." He returned, taking the second guest chair instead of sitting behind his desk. "I love conversations that start out like this."

Hunter smiled in return. "Tell me if I'm out of line."

"We're off the record," said Ethan. "You can get out of line."

"What do you think of Chantal Charbonnet?"

Ethan sat back. "Sly, but not brilliant. Gorgeous, of course. Roger seems to have noticed her."

"She was at the Bergdorf's promotion this afternoon."

"Yeah?" asked Ethan. "That's a stretch for her job description."

"It got me wondering," confided Hunter. "Why was she there?"

"Eye candy?"

"Women were the target demographic." Hunter had been thinking about this all the way over.

"Maybe she asked Roger really, really nicely?"

Hunter had considered that, too. But he didn't have evidence to support favoritism. He was coming at this from another angle. "Could she have been a role model for the consumers?"

Ethan considered the idea. "There's no denying she knows how to wear our products."

"Lays it on a bit thick, wouldn't you say?"

Ethan grinned. "My kind of consumer. We want them all to apply it like Chantal."

Ethan's words validated the worry that was niggling at Hunter's brain. Chantal was dead center on the new target demographic. Hunter was worried that Roger had seen that in her, and it wasn't something he'd seen in Sinclair. Sinclair was a lot of things—a lot of very fabulous, fun, exciting things—but she wasn't a poster child for Lush Beauty Products.

He filed away the information and switched gears. "Did Sinclair mention her spa plan to you?"

Ethan nodded. "Had lots of potential. But I hear it went south with Millennium."

"I'm going to try to revive it."

"I hope you can. If you secure the outlet, we can provide the product."

"Including lavender."

"Got it covered."

"Do you have any thoughts on a spa release overall?"

Ethan stretched out his legs, obviously speculating how frank he could be with Hunter.

Hunter waited. He wanted frank, but there was no way to insist on it.

"If it was me," said Ethan. "I wouldn't target a single spa, I'd go for the whole chain. And I'd try for the Crystal. The Millennium is nice, but the Crystal has the best overseas locations."

Hunter didn't disagree with Ethan's assessment. The Crystal Spa chain was as top of the line as they came.

"You get into Rome and Paris," said Ethan. "At that level. You'll really have some momentum."

"Tall order."

Ethan brought his hands down on his thighs. "Osland International usually shy away from a challenge?"

"Nope," said Hunter. When he was involved, Osland International always stepped up to the plate.

He could already feel his competitive instincts kick in. Although he'd come into the job reluctantly, making Lush Beauty a runaway success had inched its way to the top of his priority list.

He also knew he wanted Sinclair as a partner in this. He liked the way she thought. He liked her energy and her outside-the-box thinking. And, well, okay, and he just plain liked her. But there was nothing wrong with that. Liking your business associates was important.

All his best business relationships were based on mutual respect. Sure, maybe he didn't want to sleep with his other business associates. But the principle was the same.

Sinclair hit the buzzer, letting Hunter into the building.

She didn't know whether she'd been brilliant or stupid to take him up on his offer to paint, but there was no turning back now.

She'd dressed in a pair of old torn blue jeans and a grainy gray T-shirt with "Stolen From the New York City Police Department" emblazoned across the front. Her hair was braided tight against her head, and she'd popped a white painter's cap on her head. She had no worries that the tone of the evening would be sexy in any way.

The bell rang, echoing through the high-ceilinged, empty room. Her living room furniture was in storage for another week. But she'd already finished the small bedroom, so it was back together.

She opened the front door and the hinges groaned loudly in the cavernous space as Hunter walked in.

"Nice," he said, looking around at the tarp-draped counters and breakfast bar, the plastic on the floors, and the dangling pieces of masking tape around the bay window.

"It has a lot of potential," she told him, closing and locking the oak door. There was no doubt it was smaller than he'd be used to, but she was excited about living here.

"I wasn't being sarcastic, honest." He held up a bottle of wine. "Housewarming."

"That might be a bit premature." She still had a lot of work to get done.

He glanced around the room for somewhere to set the bottle down. "In a cupboard?" he asked, heading for the alcove kitchen.

"Beside the fridge," she called.

He got rid of the wine and shrugged out of his windbreaker. Then he returned to the main room in a pair of khakis and a white T-shirt that were obviously brand-new.

She tried not to smile at the outfit.

It really was nice of him to come and help. Still, she wasn't about to pass up an opportunity to tease him.

"You don't do home maintenance often, do you?"

He glanced around the tarp-draped room. "I've seen it done on TV."

"It's not as easy as it looks," she warned.

He shot her an expression of mock disbelief. "I have an MBA from Harvard."

"And they covered house painting in graduate school?"

"They covered macroeconomics and global capitalism."

She fought a grin. "Oh sure, go ahead and get snooty on me."

"Dip the brush and stroke it on the wall. Am I close?"

"I guess you might as well give it a try."

"Give it a *try?*"

Her grin broadened at his insulted tone.

He bent over and pried open a paint can. "You might want to shift your attitude. I'm free labor, baby."

"Am I getting what I paid for?"

"Sassy," he said, and her heart tripped a beat.

"You need to shake it," she told him, battling the sensual memory. He'd called her sassy in Manchester. In a way that said he wanted her bad.

"Shake it?" he interrupted her thoughts.

She swallowed. "You need to shake the paint before you open the can."

He raised his brow as he crouched to tap the lid back down. "You're enjoying this, aren't you?"

"You bet. Nothing like keeping the billionaire humble."

"Don't stereotype. I'm always humble."

"Yeah. I noticed that right off, Mr. Macroeconomics and Global Capitalism."

"Well, what did you take in college?"

She hesitated for a second then admitted it. "MBA. Yale."

"So, *you* took macroeconomics and global capitalism?"

"Magna cum laude," she said with a hoity toss of her head.

"Yet you can still paint. Imagine that."

She glanced at him for a moment, trying to figure out why he hadn't escalated the joke by teasing her about the designation. Then it hit her. "You got summa, at least, didn't you?"

He didn't answer.

"Geek," she said.

He grinned as he shook the paint. Then he poured it into the tray.

She broke out the brushes, and he quickly caught on to

using the long-handled roller. Sinclair cut in the corners, and together they worked their way down the longest wall.

"What do you think of the Crystal Spa chain?" he asked as his roller swished up and down in long strokes.

"I've never been there," said Sinclair from the top of the step ladder. This close to the ceiling lights, she was starting to sweat. She finally gave in and peeled off her cap.

Wisps of strands had come loose from her braid. Probably she'd end up with cream-colored specks in her hair. Whatever. They were painting her walls, not dancing in a ballroom.

"You want to try it?"

She paused at the end of her stroke, glancing down at him. Was he talking about the Crystal Spa? "Try what?"

"I was thinking, we shouldn't let the Millennium's refusal stop us. We should consider other spas."

Was he serious? More importantly, why hadn't she thought of that?

She felt a shimmer of excitement. Maybe her spa idea wasn't dead, after all. And the New York-based Crystal Spa chain would be an even better choice than the Millennium.

She'd learned from the Millennium experience. She'd make sure she was even better prepared for a pitch to the Crystal.

"Can I try out the Crystal on my expense account?" she asked with a teasing lilt.

"Of course."

Scoffing her dismissal, she went back to painting. "Like Roger would ever go for that."

Besides, she didn't have to test out the Crystal Spa to know it was fantastic. Everyone always raved.

"Forget Roger, will you?" urged Hunter. "Here."

She glanced back down.

With the roller hooked under one arm, he pulled out his wallet. Then he tossed a credit card onto her tarp-covered breakfast bar. "Consider this your expense account."

She nearly fell off the ladder. "You can't—"

"I just did."

"But—"

"Shut up." He went back to the paint tray. "I know the spa idea's great. You know the spa idea's great. Let's streamline the research and make it happen."

"You can't pay for my spa treatments."

"Osland International can pay for them. It's my corporate card, and I consider it a perfectly legitimate R & D expense."

Sinclair didn't know what to say to that. Trying out the spa would be great research, but still...

He rolled the next section. "It's not like I can go in there and check out the wax room myself."

She cringed, involuntarily flinching. "Wax room?"

He chuckled at her expression. "Buck up, Sinclair. Take one for the team."

"You take one for the team."

"I've done my part. It's my credit card."

"They're my legs."

"Who said anything about legs?"

She stared at him. He didn't. He wouldn't.

"We were this close!" She made a tiny space with her thumb and index finger. "*This* close to having a totally professional conversation."

"I'm weak," he admitted.

"You're hopeless."

"Yeah. Well. Irrespective of what you get waxed, and whether or not you show me, it's still a good idea."

It was a good idea. And her gaze strayed to his platinum

card sitting on the canvas tarp. Even if he couldn't keep his mind on business, this was not an opportunity she was about to give up. "I'm thinking a facial."

"Whatever you want. I need to know if they can deliver the kind of opportunity we're looking for."

"What if they're locked into a supplier contract like the Millennium?"

Hunter shrugged. "Every business is different. We'll deal with that when and if it happens. Tomorrow good for you?"

She nodded.

With only twelve days until Valentine's Day. There was no time to lose.

Three

The next day, lying on her back in uptown Manhattan's Crystal Spa, a loose silky robe covering her naked body, Sinclair was feeling very relaxed after her facial massage. A smooth, cool mask was drying on her face. Damp pads protected her eyes, and she found herself nearly falling asleep.

"Sinclair?"

She was dreaming of Hunter's voice. That was fine. Dreaming never hurt anybody.

"Sinclair?" the voice came again.

No.

No way.

Hunter was *not* in this room.

Warm hands closed up the wide V of her robe. "No sense playing with fire," he said.

"What are you doing here?"

"I need permission to cancel your appointments for this afternoon."

She tried to form words, but they jumbled in her brain and turned into incomprehensive sputters.

"We need to fly to L.A.," Hunter told her matter-of-factly.

"This is a dream, right? You're not really here."

"Oh, I'm really here. But, hold on, are you saying you dream about me?"

"Nightmares. Trust me."

He chuckled. "The only appointment I could get with the president of Crystal Spas was in their head office in L.A. at three today. We have to get going."

She blinked. Why did they need to talk to the president?

"I want to pitch the idea of debuting the whole chain."

Sinclair gave her head a little shake. "Seriously?"

"Yes, seriously."

They were going to debut Luscious Lavender in the entire Crystal chain? That would be a phenomenal feat.

"I could kiss you," she breathed.

"Bad idea. For the obvious reasons." Then he looked her up and down. "Plus, you're kind of…goopy."

She just grinned.

"It's not a done deal yet," he warned.

"But we are going to try."

"We are going to try. Can I cancel your appointments?"

"You got a cell phone?"

He pulled it out of his suit pocket.

She dialed Amber's number.

The whole chain. She could barely believe it. The whole damn chain.

* * *

Hunter was sorry now that he'd even told Sinclair about Crystal Spas. The meeting hadn't gone well, and she was clearly disappointed as she climbed into the jet for the return trip to New York.

"We knew it was a long shot," she said bravely, buckling up across from him.

"I'm sorry."

"It's not your fault. Some people can't make quick decisions."

The whole thing had frustrated the hell out of Hunter.

"At his level, the man had better learn to make quick decisions. He had a chance to get in on the ground floor in this."

"His loss," said Sinclair with conviction.

"They're superior products," replied Hunter.

"Of *course* they're superior products," she agreed.

Hunter did up his own seat belt. "We say emphatically as two people who've never tried them."

She smiled at his joke.

"We should try them," he said.

"I'm not trying the wax."

He chuckled. "I'll try the wax."

"Yeah, right."

"Right here." He pointed to his chest. "I'll be a man about it. You can rip my hair out by the roots if I can massage your neck with the lavender oil."

She stared into his eyes as the jet engines whined to life. "You don't think we'd end up naked within five minutes?"

"I don't think your ripping the hair from my chest would make me want to get naked."

She obviously fought a grin. "Waxing your chest is probably the worst idea I've ever heard."

"But it cheered you up."

She sighed, and some of the humor went out of her eyes. "Crystal Spas would have been perfect."

He reached for her hand. "I know."

The jet jerked to rolling, and he experienced a strong sense of déjà vu. It took him a second to realize it was Kristy, Kristy and Jack on this same airplane. During their emergency landing in Vegas, Jack had held Kristy's hand to comfort her.

Right now, Sinclair's hand felt small in Hunter's, soft and smooth. The kind of hand a man wanted all over his body.

"You want to go see your sister?" he asked.

Sinclair looked startled. "What?"

"She's in Manchester. It's on the way."

"We'd be too late."

She had a point.

"Maybe not," he argued. A visit with Kristy might cheer Sinclair up.

"Thanks for the thought."

Hunter wished he had more to offer than just a thought. But then she smiled her gratitude. Hunter realized that was what mattered.

Business deals would come and go. He'd simply find another way to make Sinclair happy. Even as the thought formed in his mind, he realized it was dangerous. But he ignored the warning flash.

"You don't need to worry about me," she told him. "I'm a big girl. And I still have the ball to plan."

"The ball's going to be fantastic," he enthused. "It'll be the best Valentine's ball anybody ever put on anywhere."

"I hate it when people humor me."

"Then why are you still smiling?"

"Because sometimes you can be very sweet."

"Hold that thought," he teased, and he brought her hand to his lips.

"I'm not going to sleep with you." She retrieved her hand, but the smile grew wider. "But, maybe, if you're very, very good, I might dance with you at the Valentine's ball."

"And maybe if you're very, very good, I might bring you flowers and candy."

"Something to look forward to."

"Isn't it?"

They both stopped talking, and a soft silence settled around the hum of the engines as they taxied toward the runway.

"It's just that we've worked day and night on this product launch," she said, half to herself.

"I can imagine," he responded with a nod.

"All of us," she added. "The Luscious Lavender products are strong. The sales force is ready. And marketing showed me a fantastic television commercial last week. I really want to make sure I do my part."

"You are doing your part." He had no doubt of that. "There's still the ball."

She gave a shrug and tucked her hair behind her ears. "The ball's pretty much ready to go. I know it'll be fine. But I wanted that something extra, that something special from the PR department." Then she sighed. "Maybe it's just ego."

"Contributing to the team is not ego. Taking all the glory is ego."

"Wanting recognition is a form of ego," she countered.

"Wanting recognition for a job well done is human."

Her voice went soft. "Then I guess I don't want to be human."

He watched her for a silent minute, trying to gauge how

deep that admission went. For all her bravado, he sensed an underlying insecurity. What Sinclair presented and who she really was were two different things. She was far more sensitive than she showed.

In the privacy and intimacy of the plane, he voiced a question that had been nagging at him for a while. "Why did you sleep with me?"

She startled and retrieved her hand. Then her shell went back into place. "Why did *you* sleep with me?"

"Because you were funny and smart and beautiful," he said. Then he waited.

"And, because I said yes?" she asked.

He didn't respond to her irreverence. "And because when I held you in my arms, it was where you belonged."

She stayed silent, and he could almost see the war going on inside her head.

"You going to tell me?" he asked.

"It was Christmas," she finally began. "And you were fun, and sexy. And Kristy had just married Jack. And life at your amazing mansion is really very surreal."

She'd buried the truth. He was sure of it.

Kristy had married Jack, and for that brief moment in time, Sinclair had felt abandoned. And there had been Hunter. And she'd clung to him. And that's what it was. He was glad he knew.

Even though he shouldn't, he switched seats so he was beside her. He wanted to be the one she clung to.

She stiffened, watching him warily.

"The steward's only a few feet away," he assured her. "Nothing can happen."

His reassurance seemed to work.

She relaxed, and he took her hand once again.

The cabin lights dimmed, the engines wound out, and the plane accelerated along the runway, pushing them back against their seats. Hunter turned his head to watch her profile, rubbed his thumb against her soft palm and inhaled her perfume, as he captured and held a moment in time.

The next morning, for the first time in her life, Sinclair came late to the office.

Amber jumped up from her desk, looking worried. "What happened?"

"I got home really late," she said as she passed by.

"Roger was down here. He wanted your files on the Valentine's ball."

Sinclair crossed the threshold to her office, dropping her briefcase and purse on her credenza, and picked up a stack of mail on the way to her desk. "Why?"

"So *Chantal* could review them."

"What?" She stared at Amber. "Why would she do that?"

"Because she's queen of the freakin' universe? Is there something I should know, Sinclair? Something pertaining to PR?"

"No." Sinclair set down the mail. "There's nothing for you to worry about." She moved to the door. "Wait here."

"I'm not going anywhere."

"I assume you gave him the files?" Sinclair called over her shoulder.

"I didn't have a choice."

No. She didn't.

When the president asked for the files, you gave up the files. But there was nothing saying you didn't go get them back again. Roger's micromanaging was getting out of hand. So was Chantal's apparent carte blanche in the PR department. Sinclair took a tight breath, pressed the button, and waited as the elevator ascended.

This inserting of Chantal into Sinclair's projects had to stop. You didn't add a new voice ten days before the ball. And you sure didn't empower a neophyte like Chantal on a project of this size and importance.

What was the matter with Roger? Was he trying to sabotage Sinclair's efforts?

Maybe it was due to her frustration over the failure of the spa plan, but Sinclair was feeling exceedingly protective of the ball. It was her one chance for the PR department to shine, and she was determined to do it or die trying.

The doors slid open on twenty, revealing burgundy carpet, soft lighting and cherrywood paneling. Myra, Roger's secretary, looked surprised to see her.

"Did you have an appointment?"

"I need two minutes with Roger."

Myra glanced at Roger's door. "I'm afraid he's—"

The office door opened.

Chantal Charbonnet stepped out, a stack of files tucked under her arm. She was wearing a leather skirt today, with a glittering gold blouse. Her heels were high, her neckline low. She gave Sinclair a disdainful look and passed by with a sniff of her narrow pert nose

"Looks like he's free," said Sinclair.

Myra picked up the phone. "Let me just—"

"I'll only take a second." Sinclair didn't give the woman a chance to stop her.

Before Roger's door could swing shut, she blocked it. "Excuse me, Roger?"

He glanced up, lips compressing, and a furrow forming in the middle of his brow.

"I don't recall a meeting," he said.

"I believe you have my files?"

"Chantal's taking a look at them."

Sinclair struggled hard to keep her voice even. "May I ask why?"

"I've asked her to provide her opinion."

"On?"

"On the Valentine's ball preparation. She's taking a bigger role in the new product launch. I think we all recognize Chantal's talents."

Well, Sinclair sure didn't recognize Chantal's talents. And the ball preparations were all but done. She just needed to babysit it for the next week and a half. She sure didn't need somebody messing with the plans at this late date.

Roger took in her expression, and his tone suddenly turned syrupy. "I appreciate how hard you've been working, Sinclair. And I know you're busy. This will take some of the burden off your shoulders."

"There's no—"

"You'll get your files back in a couple of days. Thanks for stopping by."

Thanks for stopping by?

He'd pulled the most interesting and important project of her career out from under her, and *that's* all she got?

Short of a raid on Chantal's office, Sinclair didn't know what to do. If the woman started messing with things, the ball could be completely destroyed. What if she called Claude at the Roosevelt? The head chef was temperamental at the best of times, and Chantal might push him right over the edge.

The conductor also needed hand-holding. The music was cued to coincide with speeches and product giveaways. Entrances and exits of VIPs were specifically timed, and the media appointments had to come off like clockwork.

But Sinclair couldn't outright defy Roger.

She headed for the elevator, desperately cataloguing potential problems and possible solutions. By the time she punched the button, she realized there were too many variables. With a rising sense of panic, she knew she couldn't possibly save the ball from Chantal. That left her with Roger. How could she possibly make Roger understand the danger of Chantal?

She entered the elevator, then froze with her finger on the button.

Wait a minute. She had this all wrong. She shouldn't be fighting them. What better way to demonstrate the error in their thinking than to go along with it? Ms. Chantal wanted to take over the ball? She could bloody well take over the ball. It would take less than twenty-four hours for her to get into a mess. Sinclair wouldn't argue with the president. She'd graciously step aside. She'd take the day off and leave Chantal with just enough rope to hang herself.

When Sinclair came back tomorrow, hopefully they'd be ready to listen to reason. As the elevator dropped, Sinclair drew a deep, bracing breath.

It was all but suicidal. But it would be worth it.

Ha!

Roger wanted to give Chantal a chance to shine? Sinclair would graciously step aside. When she came back tomorrow, hopefully they'd be ready to listen to reason.

As the elevator dropped, Sinclair warmed to the idea. When she got back to her office, she informed Amber they'd have the files back in a couple of days, and that she was going home to paint.

* * *

A few hours later, with U2 blaring in the background, Sinclair's frustration had translated itself into a second coat on most of one wall. She was busy at one corner of the ceiling when there was a banging on the door.

She climbed down the ladder and set her brush on the edge of the paint tray.

The banging came again.

"I'm coming," she called. She wiped off her hands, then pulled open the door.

It was Hunter, and he was carrying a large shopping bag.

"I've been buzzing you downstairs for ten minutes." He marched across the room and turned down the music. "Thank goodness for the lady on the first floor walking her dog."

"I was busy," said Sinclair.

Hunter dropped the bag onto the plastic-covered floor. "What happened?"

"I decided I should spend the day painting my living room."

"I talked to Amber."

Sinclair shrugged, picking up her paintbrush, and mounting the ladder. "What did she tell you?"

"That you were painting your living room instead of working."

"See that?" she gestured to the brushes, paint cans and tarps. "All evidence points to exactly the same thing. I am, in fact, painting my living room."

"She also told me you haven't taken a day off in eight years."

Sinclair dipped the brush in the can on the ladder and stroked along the top of the wall. "Meaning I'm due."

"Meaning you're upset."

"A girl can't get upset?"

He crossed his arms over his chest. "What happened?"

"Nothing much." The important thing now was to get the painting done, then go in tomorrow and see if her plan had worked.

"Do I have to come up there and get you?"

She laughed, dabbing the brush hard against the masking tape in the corner. "Now that would be interesting."

"Quit messing around, Sinclair."

She sighed in defeat. Being micromanaged was embarrassing. "You want to know?" she asked.

"Yes," said Hunter. "I want to know."

"Roger gave Chantal my Valentine's Day ball files. She needed to review them because, apparently, we've *all* recognized her *talents*."

"We have?"

Sinclair dipped the brush again. "Therefore, she's ready to be the PR assistant. No. Wait. I think she's ready to be the PR manager."

"What exactly did Roger say?"

"Not much. He just gave her the files. He seems hell-bent on involving her in every aspect of my job."

"Oh."

There was something in Hunter's tone.

Sinclair stopped painting and looked down. "What?"

He took a breath then paused.

"What?" she repeated.

"There's something we should discuss."

"You know what's going on?"

"Maybe."

Sinclair took a step down the ladder. "Hunter?"

He dropped his arms to his sides. "I have a theory. It's only a theory."

She climbed the rest of the way down. "What is it?"

Hunter took the brush from her hand, setting it on the paint tray just before it dripped on the floor. "Chantal asked if you used the mousse."

He lifted the shopping bag. "I think that might be what Roger's picking up on. Chantal's, well, pizzazz."

A sick feeling slid into Sinclair's stomach.

Roger thought Chantal knew better than Sinclair?

Hunter thought Chantal knew better than Sinclair?

"You have to admit," Hunter continued. "She's the demographic Luscious Lavender is targeting."

"You sure you want to keep on talking?"

"We both know she's not you. We both know you're smart and talented and hard working."

"Well, thank you for that."

He opened the bag to reveal the full gamut of Luscious Lavender products. "I think you should try these out. See what you think, maybe—"

"Right. Because all my problems will be solved by a good shampoo and mousse." Her problem wasn't a bad hair day. It was the fact that Roger, and maybe Hunter, too, preferred beauty over brains.

Hunter attempted a grin. "Don't forget waxing."

She reached down for the paintbrush. "I'm forgetting all of it."

"Will you at least hear me out?"

"No." Without thinking she waved the brush for emphasis, and paint splattered on the front of his suit.

Her eyes went wide in horror. "Oh, I'm so sorry," she quickly blurted out.

"Forget it."

"But I ruined your suit." She could only imagine how much it had cost.

"I said to forget it."

How was she supposed to hang on to her moral outrage when he was being a gentleman?

"It's more than just a good shampoo," he said. "It's about relating to your customers. Having your customers relate to you."

She started up the ladder.

"They relate to Chantal in a particular way," he said. "They see her look as an idealized version of themselves. These are people that put great stock in the value of beauty products to their lives, and they want to know that you put great stock in them, as well."

"You're suggesting I could replace an MBA and eight years of experience with a good makeover?"

What kind of a man would think that?

"Yes," he said.

She stopped. She couldn't believe he'd actually said it out loud.

"But," he continued. "I'm also suggesting you'll blow the competition out of the water when you have both."

"You think Chantal is my competition?"

"I think *Roger* thinks she's your competition. I think you could do a makeover with your eyes closed. And I think she's only a threat to you if you let her be a threat to you."

"So *I'm* choosing to have this happen?"

All she'd ever done was her job. She'd shown up early every day for eight years. She'd written speeches and press releases, planned events, supported her coworkers, solved problems and taken the message of Lush Beauty far and wide. If her performance evaluations were anything to go by, she'd been more than successful in her role as PR manager.

"You're choosing not to fight it," said Hunter.

"I shouldn't have to fight it." When had hard work and success stopped being enough?

"Too bad. So sad. Are you going to let her win?" He paused. "Do you *want* your career path to end?"

"Don't be ridiculous." She loved her job.

"I'm the one being ridiculous? Chantal's nipping at your heels, and *I'm* the one being ridiculous?"

"Why do you care?"

There were a few seconds of silence. "Why do you think I care?"

Sinclair didn't have an answer for that, so she finished climbing the ladder.

"I'm not saying it's right," he spoke below her. "I'm saying that's the business you're in. And you're the PR manager. And, yes, I'm sorry, but it matters. And, as for why I care."

He stopped talking, and she held her breath.

"I like you? I slept with you? You're an asset to Lush Beauty? You're family? Take your pick. But I'm about done fighting, Sinclair. If you don't want my help, I'm out of here."

She dipped her paintbrush, feeling hollow and exhausted. Hunter's words pulsed in her ears, while paint dribbles dried on her hands. She pretended to focus on the painting while she waited for the door to slam behind him.

Emotion stung her eyes.

She didn't mean to fight with him.

It wasn't his fault that Chantal was prancing around the city like a poster child for Luscious Lavender. It wasn't his fault that Roger was interfering in her management of the PR department. And what did Sinclair want from Hunter, anyway? For him to intervene with Roger?

Not.

She could take care of her own professional life.

Sort of. Maybe.

Because a tiny, little voice inside her told her some of what Hunter said made sense.

She focused on the paint, stroking it into the corner, listening for his footfalls, for the door slamming, for him walking out of her life.

"I'm sorry," his unexpected words came from behind and below her. "I should have approached that differently."

She stopped midstroke. Shocked, relieved and embarrassed all at the same time. She set down the brush.

"No," she spoke to the wall. "I'm the one who's sorry."

Silence.

"Will you come down then?"

She gave a shaky nod. She couldn't bring herself to look at him as she started down the ladder. Maybe all of what he said made sense. Maybe she'd been hasty in dismissing a makeover. After all, what could it hurt to try?

What exactly was the principle she was standing on? She'd always wanted the world to take her seriously. She hadn't wanted a free ride because of looks and glamour. But did she want to put herself at a disadvatange?

"I suppose," she said as her foot touched the floor and she turned toward him. "It wouldn't kill me to try the shampoo."

"That a girl." His voice was full of approval.

"It's just that I never wanted to cheat," she tried to explain. "I never wanted to wonder if a promotion or a pay raise, or even people's reactions to me were because of my looks."

"You're not cheating. You're leveling the playing field. Besides, being beautiful has nothing to do with makeup and mousse." He shrugged out of the ruined jacket and tossed it on the floor. He whipped off his tie. "You're beautiful, Sinclair. And there's not a damn thing you can do about it."

Her heartbeat thickened in her chest, wondering what would come off next.

But he rolled up his sleeves. "Okay, let's get to work."

That threw her. "We're going to the office?"

"We're painting your walls."

"You want to spend the afternoon here?"

"You bet."

By late afternoon, Sinclair's arms were about to fall off. Her shoulders ached, and she was getting a headache from the paint fumes. Her latest can was empty, so she climbed down the ladder to replace it.

Hunter appeared, taking the can from her hands.

"You're done," he said.

"There's another whole wall."

He pointed across the room. "See that bag over there? Full of bath oil, shampoo and gel?"

"Uh-huh."

"I want you to take it into the bathroom and run a very hot, very deep bath. In fact—" he set down the paint can and propped up his roller "—I'll do it for you."

Before she could protest, he picked up the shopping bag and marched into the bathroom.

She heard the fan go on and the water gush from the faucet. She knew any self-respecting woman would fight against his high-handed behavior. But, honestly, she was just too tired.

After a few minutes, he returned to the living room. He didn't talk, just unplugged her CD player and gathered up the two compact speakers. He popped out U2 and replaced it with Norah Jones.

Then he was back to the bathroom.

Curiosity finally got the better of her, and she wandered in to find her tub full of steaming, foamy water, and three cinnamon-scented candles flickering at the base of the tub. They'd been a Christmas gift from somebody at the office. But she'd never used them.

"I never have baths," she admitted.

"Why not?"

"Showers are more efficient."

"But baths are more fun."

"You have baths, do you?" she couldn't help but tease.

He faced her in the tiny room. "Guys don't take baths. They want girls to take them. It makes them all soft and warm, and in the mood to get beautiful."

She gave a mock sigh. "It's time-consuming being all girly."

He grinned. "Piece of cake being a guy."

"Double standard."

"You know it."

"Still." She glanced down at the steaming water. "It does look inviting."

"That's because it is." He reached across her shoulder and flicked off the light.

"Time to take off your clothes," he rumbled.

A sensual shiver ran through her, and she reflexively reached for the hem of her T-shirt.

But his large hands closed over hers to stop them. "I mean after I leave."

"You're leaving?"

He kissed her forehead. "I didn't come here to seduce you, Sinclair."

Suddenly, she wished he had.

"Don't look at me like that. I'm going to paint for a while, or we'll never finish."

"I can paint later."

His finger brushed over her lips to silence her. "The price of being a guy. Your mission is to get all glammed up and frou frou. My mission is to give you the time to do that."

Then he winked, and left the room, clicking the door shut behind him. And Sinclair shifted her attention to the deep, claw-footed tub.

It looked decadently wonderful. He'd set out the shampoo, bath gel and lotion. And he'd obviously poured some of the Luscious Lavender foaming oil into the water. She'd spent the last six months thinking about the artsy labels, the expensive magazine ads, the stuffed sample gift baskets for the ball, and the retail locations that needed some extra attention promotions-wise. Funny, that she'd never thought much about the products themselves.

The water steamed, and the lavender scent filled the room, and the anticipation of that luxurious heat on her aching shoulders was more than tempting.

She peeled off her T-shirt, unzipped her jeans, then slipped out of her underwear. She eased, toe-first, into the scorching bathwater, dipping in her foot, her calf, her knee. Then she slowly brought in her other foot, bracing her hands on the edges of the tub to lower her body into the hot water.

After her skin grew accustomed to the temperature, and her shoulders and neck began to sigh in pleasure, her thoughts made their way to Hunter. He was on the other side of that thin wall. And she was naked. And he knew she was naked.

She pictured him opening the door, wearing nothing but a smile, a glass of wine in each hand. He'd cross the black and white tiles, bend to kiss her, maybe on the neck, maybe on the lips. He'd set down their glasses. Then he'd draw her to her feet, dripping wet, the scented oil slick on her skin. His hands would roam over her stomach, her breasts, her buttocks, pulling her tight against his body, lifting her—

Something banged outside and Hunter swore in frustration. Clearly, he wasn't out there stripping off his clothes and popping the wine cork. She was naked, not twenty feet away, and he was dutifully painting.

She sucked in a breath and ducked her head under the water.

Four

By the time Sinclair emerged from her bathroom, wrapped in a thick, terry robe, her face glowing, her wet hair combed back from her face, Hunter had cleaned up the paint and ordered a pizza. The smell of tomatoes and cheese wafted up from the cardboard box on the breakfast bar while he popped the cork from his housewarming bottle of wine.

"How did you know sausage and mushroom is my favorite?" she asked as she padded across the paint splattered tarps.

"I'm psychic." He retrieved two stools from beneath the tarp, then opened the top of the pizza box.

"How'd it go in there?" he asked her, watching her climb up on one stool.

She arranged the robe so that it covered her from head to toe, and he tried not to think about what was under there.

She smiled in a way that did his heart good. "I'm a whole new woman."

"Not completely new, I hope," he teased as he took the stool facing her. The covered breakfast bar was at their elbows.

She grinned. "Don't worry. I saved the best parts."

"Oh, good." He poured them each a glass of the pinot. "So, are you ready to move on to makeup?"

She reached for a slice of pizza. "You planning to help me with that, too?"

He took in her straggled hair, squeaky clean face and oversized robe. If he had his way, he'd keep her exactly as she was. But this wasn't about him.

"I don't think you want to arm me with a mascara wand."

"But you've done such a good job so far." She blinked her thick lashes ingenuously.

"We could call one of the Bergdorf ladies."

She waved a dismissive hand. "I'll be fine."

"You sure?"

She hit him with an impatient stare. "It's not that I *can't* put on a lot of makeup. It's that I *don't* put on a lot of makeup."

"Oh."

She chewed on her slice of pizza, and he followed suit. After a while, she slipped her bare feet off the stool's crossbar and swung them in the air while they ate in companionable silence.

"What about clothes?" he asked.

"I'll call Kristy and get some suggestions."

He nodded his agreement. Having a sister in the fashion design business had to help. "Sounds like you've got everything handled," he observed.

She shifted on the stool, flexing her neck back and forth, wincing. "It's not going to be that big of a deal. I'm a pretty efficient project manager. The only difference is, this time the project is me."

Hunter wasn't convinced project management was the right approach. There was something in the art and spirit of beauty she seemed to be missing. But he was happy to have got her this far, and he wasn't about to mess with his success.

She lifted her wineglass and the small motion caused her to flinch in obvious pain.

He motioned for her to turn around.

She glanced behind her. "What?"

"Go ahead. Turn." He motioned again, and this time she complied.

"You painted too long," he told her as he loosened her robe on her neck and pressed his thumbs into the stiff muscles on her shoulders.

"I wanted to finish."

"You're going to be sore in the morning." He found a knot and began to work it.

"I'll live. Mmmmm."

"That's the spot?"

"Oh, yeah."

He'd promised himself he'd stick to business, and he would. But his body had reacted the instant he'd touched her. Her skin was warm from the bath, slick from the bath oil, and fragrant from the water and the candles. But he scooted his stool closer, persisting in the massage, determined to keep this all about her.

To distract himself, he glanced around at the freshly painted room. It was small, but the windows were large, and he could see that it had potential to be cozy and inviting. In fact, he preferred it to the big, Osland family house on Long Island.

He stayed there whenever he was in town, but with just him and a couple of staff members, it always seemed to echo with emptiness. Right now, he wished he could invite Sinclair over to fill it up with laughter. "Have you always lived in New York?" he asked her instead.

She nodded. "Kristy and I went to school in Brooklyn. You?"

"Mostly in California."

"Private school, I bet."

"You're right."

"Uniforms and everything?"

"Yes."

She tipped her head to glance up at him. "You must have looked cute in your little short pants and tie."

"I'm sure I was adorable." He dug his thumb into a stubborn knot in her shoulder.

"Ouch. Was that for calling you cute?"

"That was to make you feel better in the morning."

She flexed her shoulder under his hands. "Did you by any chance play football in high school?"

"Soccer and basketball. You?"

"I edited the school newspaper."

"Nerdy."

"Exciting. I once covered a murder."

He paused. "There was a murder at your high school?"

She gave a long, sad sigh of remembrance. "Mrs. Mitchell's goldfish. Its poor, lifeless body was found on the science table. Someone had cruelly removed it from its tank after hours. We suspected the janitor."

Hunter could picture an earnest, young Sinclair hot on the trail of a murder suspect, all serious and no-nonsense, methodically reviewing the evidence.

"Did he do it?" Hunter asked.

"We couldn't prove it. But it was the best headline we ever had. Broke the record for copy sales." She sounded extremely proud of the accomplishment.

"You were definitely a nerd," he said.

"I prefer the term intellectual."

"I bet you ran in the school election."

"True."

"There you go." He'd made his point.

"Billy Jones beat me out for class president in ninth grade." She put a small catch in her voice. "I was crushed. I never ran again."

"I'd have voted for you," said Hunter.

"No. Like everyone else, you'd have fallen for Billy's chocolate coconut snowballs—"

"His *what?*"

"Chocolate and coconut on the outside, marshmallow cream on the inside. He brought five boxes to school and handed them out during his speech. I didn't have a chance."

"Marshmallow cream, you say?"

Sinclair elbowed him in the chest. "Quit salivating back there."

"I'd still have voted for you."

"Liar."

He chuckled at her outrage and eased her back against his body. "Oh, I'd have eaten the snowball. But it's a secret ballot, right?"

"Traitor." But her muscles relaxed under his hands, and her body grew more pliant.

Finally, he stopped massaging and wrapped his arms around her waist. "I bet you were a cute little nerd."

She rested her head against his chest. He didn't dare move. He barely dared breathe. All it would take was one kiss, and he'd be dragging her off to the bedroom.

She tipped her head to look up at him, all sweetness and vulnerability.

"Hunter?" she breathed, lips dark and parted, eyes filled with passion and desire.

He closed his, fighting like hell to keep from kissing her lips. "I don't want to be that guy," he told her, discovering how true that was. Because he didn't want to screw up their budding friendship.

"That guy?"

"That guy with the bath and the candles and the shoulder massage."

"I liked that part."

He opened his eyes again. "It's Seduction 101 for losers."

"Are you calling yourself a loser?"

"I'm saying if I make love with you, I'll feel like I cheated."

"There's a way to cheat?"

He reflexively squeezed her tight. "I cheated, and you never had a chance."

"As in, I don't know my own mind?"

"Is there an answer for that that won't get me in trouble?"

"Not really."

He ruthlessly ignored the feel of her in his arms. He wasn't willing to risk that she might regret it in the morning.

"You're tired. You're vulnerable. And we haven't thought this through. We turn that corner," he continued, "we can't turn back."

"I know," she acknowledged in a soft voice.

He leaned around her, placing a lingering kiss on her temple. "I'll see you at the office?"

"Sure."

He forced himself to let go of her. Then, using every ounce of his strength and determination, he stood up and walked away.

* * *

By 7:00 a.m., Sinclair was in her office.

After Hunter left last night, she'd lain awake, remembering his soft voice, his easy conversation, and the massage that had all but melted her muscles. She would have willingly made love with him. But, he was right. They hadn't thought it through. It was hard enough ignoring what had happened six weeks ago, never mind rekindling all those memories.

Hunter was a thoughtful man. He was also an intelligent man, and she'd spent some time going over his professional advice. He saw Chantal as her competition. And he saw Roger in Chantal's corner. Sinclair realized she had to do this, and she had to do it right. It was time to stop fooling around.

So, she'd arrived this morning with a plan to do just that. She submitted an electronic leave form, rescheduled her meetings, plastered her active files with Post-its for Amber, and left out-of-office messages on both her voice mail and e-mail.

She was working her way through the mail in her in-basket when Roger walked in.

"What's this?" he asked, dropping the leave form printout on her desk.

"I'm going on vacation," she answered cheerfully, tossing another piece of junk mail in the wastepaper basket.

"Why? Where?"

"Because I haven't taken a vacation in eight years. Because I'm entitled to vacation time just like everybody else. And because I'm not currently needed on the Valentine's Day ball file."

"Of *course* you're needed on the file."

"To do what?"

Roger waved his arms. "To make plans. To order things."

"Plans are made. Things are ordered." She rose from her

chair and smiled at him. "You'll be fine, Roger. You've got Chantal on the case. She can oversee things."

"But, where are you going?"

"Chapter Three, Section Twelve of the employee manual. Employees shall not be required to disclose nor justify their vacation plans. All efforts will be made to ensure employees are able to take leave during the time period of their choosing. And leave shall not be unreasonably withheld."

"She's right," came Hunter's voice from the doorway.

Roger looked from Hunter to Sinclair and back again. "You knew about this?"

"Hadn't a clue." Hunter looked to Sinclair. "Taking a vacation?"

"I am."

"Good for you. A refreshed employee is a productive employee."

"I plan to be refreshed," she said.

Hunter smirked. "I'm looking forward to that."

"I've left notes for Amber," Sinclair said to Roger. "The meetings with the Roosevelt Hotel have been rescheduled. Unless Chantal wants to take them. You could ask her. The florist order is nailed down. The music...Well, there's a little problem with the band, but I'm sure Chantal or Amber can handle it."

She dropped the last piece of mail in the waste basket and glanced around the room. "I think that about covers it."

"This is unexpected," said Roger through clenched teeth.

"Can I talk to you for a minute?" asked Hunter.

"My office?" Roger responded.

"I meant Sinclair," said Hunter, stepping aside from the open door.

Roger frowned.

Sinclair should have cared about his annoyance, and she should have been bothered by the fact that the CEO had just dismissed the president in order to talk to her. But she truly didn't care. She had things to do, places to go, beauticians to meet.

Roger stalked out of the office, and Hunter closed the door behind him.

"Career-wise," said Sinclair. "And by that, I mean *my* career. I'm not sure that was the best move."

"You're taking some time for the makeover?" asked Hunter.

She straightened a stack of reports and lifted them from her desktop. "You're right that Lush Beauty Products is going through a huge transition. And you're right I should thwart Roger by getting a makeover. And, honestly, I believe Roger and Chantal need some time alone to get to know one another."

Hunter grinned, obviously understanding her Machiavellian motives.

"I'm a goal-oriented woman, Hunter. Give me a week, and I can accomplish this."

"I'm sure you can. Any interest in accomplishing it in Paris?"

She squinted. She didn't understand the question.

"I had an idea," he said. He paused, obviously for effect. "The Castlebay Spa chain. It's a very exclusive, European boutique spa chain, headquartered in Paris."

She got his point and excitement shimmered through her. "We're going to try again?"

"Oslands don't quit."

Enthusiasm gathered in her chest at the thought of another shot at a spa. She squared her shoulders. "Neither do Mahoneys."

"Good to hear. Because that platinum card I gave you works in Paris."

"Oh, no." She shook her head. "You don't need me to do

the spa deal, and I don't need to go to Paris. I've got things to do in New York."

He took her hand. "I want you in on the spa deal. And Paris is the makeover capital of the world."

"Paris is definitely overkill." She didn't need to cross an ocean to get a haircut and buy dresses. Plus, in Paris, she'd be with Hunter. And there was the ever present danger of sleeping together. Since they'd so logically decided against it last night, it seemed rather cavalier to take off to Paris together.

"Do I need reinforcements? I could call your sister. She'll back me up."

"Don't you dare call Kristy." Kristy would be over the moon at the thought of a Paris makeover for her sister. And Sinclair would have two people to argue with.

He pulled out his cell phone and waggled it in the air. "She's on speed dial."

"That's cheating."

"I've got nothing against cheating."

His words from last night came back to her, but she didn't mention it.

"I need you in Paris," he said.

She didn't believe that for a second. "No, you don't."

"I need your expertise on the Castlebay deal."

She rolled her eyes. "Like my track record on spa deals is any good."

"You know the Lush Beauty company and the products, and you can describe them a lot better than I can."

"There's a flaw in this plan," she told him. But deep down inside, she knew Hunter was winning. If she wanted to beat Chantal at her own game, a Paris makeover would give her the chance she needed.

"Only flaw I can think of," he said, shifting closer, "is that I desperately want to kiss you right now."

"That's a pretty big flaw," she whispered.

"We're handling it so far." But he moved closer still, and his gaze dropped to her lips.

"How long would we be in Paris?"

"A few days."

Her lips began to tingle in reaction to his look. "Separate rooms?"

"Of course."

"Lots of time in public places."

He returned his gaze to her eyes. "Chicken."

"I'm only trying to save you from yourself."

"Noble of you."

She couldn't help but smile. "If we do this—"

"The jet's waiting at the airport."

"Did I miss the part where I said yes?"

He reached for her hand. "I'm generally one step ahead of you, Sinclair."

She shook her head, but she also grabbed her purse. Because she realized he was right. He had an uncanny knack for anticipating her actions, along with her desires.

Five

They slept on the plane, and arrived in Paris a week before Valentine's Day. Then a limousine took them to the Ciel D'Or Hotel. And Hunter insisted they get right to the makeover.

So, before Sinclair could even get her bearings, they were gazing up at the arched facade of La Petite Fleur—a famous boutique in downtown Paris. A uniformed doorman opened the gold-gilded glass door.

"Monsieur Osland," he said and tipped his hat.

Sinclair slid Hunter a smirking gaze. "Just how many makeovers do you do around here?"

"At least a dozen a year," said Hunter as their footfalls clicked on the polished marble floor.

"And here I thought I was special." They passed between two ornate pillars and onto plush, burgundy carpeting.

"You are special."

"Then how come the doorman knew you by sight? And don't try to tell me you've been shopping for Kristy."

"Like good ol' cousin Jack wouldn't kill me if I did that. They don't know me by sight. They know me because I called ahead and asked them to stay open late."

Sinclair glanced around, realizing the place was empty. "They stayed open late? Don't you think you're getting carried away here?" She'd agreed to a makeover, not to star in some remake of Pygmalion.

He chuckled. "You ain't seen nothing yet."

"Hunter."

"Shhh."

A smartly dressed woman appeared in the wide aisle and glided toward them.

"Monsieur Osland, Mademoiselle," she smiled. *"Bienvenue."*

"Bienvenue," Hunter returned. "Thank you so much for staying open for us."

The woman waved a dismissive hand. "You are most welcome, of course. We are pleased to have you."

"Je vous présente Sinclair Manhoney," said Hunter with what sounded like a perfect accent.

Sinclair held out her hand, trying very hard not to feel as if she'd dropped through the looking glass. "A pleasure to meet you."

"And you," the woman returned. "I am Jeanette. Would you care to browse? Or shall I bring out a few things?"

"We're looking for something glamorous, sophisticated but young," Hunter put in.

Jeanette nodded. "Please, this way."

She led them along an aisle, skirting a six-story atrium, to a group of peach and gold armchairs. The furniture sat on a large dais, outside a semicircle of mirrored changing rooms.

"Would either of you care for a drink?" asked Jeanette. "Some champagne?"

"Champagne would be very nice," said Hunter. "Merci."

Jeanette turned to walk away, and Hunter gestured to one of the chairs.

Sinclair dropped into it. "Overkill. Did I mention this is overkill?"

"Come on, get into the spirit of things."

"This place is…" She gestured to the furnishings, the paintings, the clothing and the atrium. "Out of my league."

"It's exactly in your league."

"You should have warned me."

"Warned you about what? That we're getting clothes? That we're getting jewelry? What part of makeover didn't you understand?"

"The part where you go bankrupt."

"You couldn't bankrupt me if you tried."

"I'm not going to try."

"Oh, please. It would be so much more fun if you did."

Jeanette reappeared, and Sinclair's attention shifted to the half a dozen assistants who followed her, carrying a colorful array of clothes.

"Those are pink," whispered Sinclair, her stomach falling. "And fuzzy. And shiny." Okay, there was makeover, and then there was comic relief.

"Time for you to go to work," said Hunter.

"Pink," she hissed at him.

Hunter just smiled.

Jeanette hung two of the outfits inside a large, well-lit changing room. It had a chair, a small padded bench, a dozen hooks and a three-way mirror.

In the changing room, Sinclair stripped out of the gray skirt suit she'd worn on the plane, and realized her underwear was looking a bit shabby. The lace on her bra had faded to ivory from the bright white it was when she'd bought it. The elastic had stretched in the straps, and one of the underwires had a small bend.

She slipped into the first dress. It was a pale pink sheath of a thing. It clung all the way to her ankles, leaving absolutely nothing to the imagination. Making matters worse, it had an elaborate beading running over the cap sleeves and all the way down the sides. And it came with a ridiculous ivory lace hood thing that made her look like some kind of android bride.

There was a small rap at the door. "Mademoiselle?"

"Yes?"

"Is there anything you need?"

Cyanide? "Would you happen to have a phone?" Or maybe an escape hatch out the back? She could catch a plane to New York and start over again.

"*Oui. Of course. Un moment.*"

Sinclair stared at the dress, having some very serious second thoughts. Maybe other women could pull this off, taller, thinner, crazier women. But it sure wasn't working for her.

Another knock.

"Yes?" If that was Hunter, she wasn't going out there. Not like this. Not with a gun to her head.

"Your phone," said Jeanette.

Sinclair pulled off the hood, cracked the door and accepted the wireless telephone.

She dialed her sister Kristy, the fashion expert.

Kristy answered after three rings. "Hello?"

"Hey, it's me."

"Hey, you," came Kristy's voice above some background

noise of music and voices. "What's going on? Everything all right?"

"It's fine. Well, not fine exactly. I'm having a few problems at work."

"Really? That's not like you. What kind of problems?"

"It's a long story. But, I'm in Paris right now, and we're trying to fix it."

"Hang on," said Kristy. "I'm at the Manchester Hospital Foundation lunch. I need to get out of the ballroom." The background noise disappeared. "Okay. There. Did you say you were in Paris?"

Sinclair's glance went to the three-way mirror. "Yes. I'm doing a makeover, but I think I many have taken a wrong turn here, and I need some advice."

"Happy to help. What kind of advice?"

"What do I ask for? Is there something that's stylish but not weird?"

"Define weird."

"At the moment, these crazy people are trying to dress me like an android bride, porn queen."

There was laughter in Kristy's tone. "Crazy people? What did you do to upset the French?"

"It's not the French. It's Hunter."

"Hunter's in Paris?"

"Yes."

Kristy was silent for a moment. "Are you sleeping with him again?"

"No."

More silence. "You sure?"

"Yes I'm sure. What? You think I wouldn't notice? We're shopping for clothes."

"I know things about Hunter that you don't."

"We're not having sex, we're shopping for clothes. And I'm all for that. Just not these clothes." Sinclair glanced in the mirror again and shuddered.

"Where are you shopping?"

"La Petite Fleur."

"Well, they're good. Is somebody assisting you?"

"Yes. A nice lady named Jeanette, who appears to have horrible taste in dresses."

"Put her on."

"Just a minute."

Sinclair cracked the door again. "Jeanette?"

"Oui?" The woman instantly appeared.

Sinclair held out the phone. "My sister wants to talk to you."

If Jeanette was surprised by the request, she didn't show it. She was gracious and classy as she took the phone, and Sinclair was grateful.

"Allô?" said Jeanette.

Sinclair closed the door. She didn't want to risk Hunter calling her to come out there.

She stripped out of the dress and tried the other. It was made of black netting, with shoulder-length matching gloves. A puffy neckline of feathers nearly made Sinclair sneeze, while rows of horizontal feather stripes camouflaged strategic parts of her body. The netting base was see-through, so underwear would be out of the question beneath it.

Another knock.

"Yes?"

"You going to show me something?" asked Hunter.

"Not a chance."

"Why? What's wrong?"

She took in her own image. Maybe she just didn't have the

body for high fashion. Other women looked good. Kristy always looked good.

"I really don't want to go into it," she said to Hunter.

"Keep an open mind. It can't be that bad."

"Trust me. It's that bad."

"Perhaps you'd care to try a different designer?" came Jeanette's voice.

"Is Kristy still on the phone?"

"She will ring you back. But she made some suggestions."

Sinclair flipped open the door latch. "No peeking," she warned Hunter.

Then his cell phone beeped and she heard him answer it.

Good. Hopefully he'd be busy for a while.

She opened the door wide enough to take the new dresses from Jeanette. They were in blues and golds, and these ones didn't appear to be pornographic.

She closed the door, took a breath, and tried on another one.

It was much better, and she felt a surge of hope.

It clung to her body, but not in an indecent way, and the fabric was thick enough that she could wear underwear beneath it. The netting on this dress was brown, and it was only used for a stripe across the top as well as a flirty ruffle from midcalf to the floor. In between was a glittering puzzle pattern of gold, brown, purple and green material.

Sinclair turned. She liked the way the ruffle flowed around her ankles, and the dress molded nicely to her rear end and her thighs.

There was another rap on the door. "How are you, madame?" called Jeanette.

Sinclair opened the door.

Jeanette cocked her head to one side. "Not bad," she said

of the outfit. "You'll need some shoes with a little jazz to compete. And maybe a little more support in your bra."

Was Sinclair offended by that last remark? No way. She was starting to like her new image.

"One moment," said Jeanette.

She returned promptly with a bra, matching panties, a pair of stockings, and some spike-heeled, precarious-looking, rhinestone-studded sandals.

When Sinclair walked out of the change room, she nearly took Hunter's breath away. The dress was a dream. Well, mostly her body beneath it was a dream. She looked glamorous and stylish, and it only added to her innate class.

"Can you hang on a minute?" he asked Richard Franklin, one of the Osland International lawyers.

"Sure," Richard responded.

Hunter covered the phone. "Perfect," he stated to Sinclair.

She smiled and, as usual, it lifted his mood. He found himself thinking about the evening ahead, and tomorrow, and the next few days. What could he show her in Paris? How could he keep her smiling?

He forced himself to switch his attention to Jeanette. "Can you do two or three more like that? And a couple of ball gowns, and some daywear?"

"Absolument."

"You look fantastic," he said to Sinclair.

It was a rocky start. But then she reflexively glanced in the mirror beside her, and he could tell by the shine in her eyes that she liked the outfit, too.

"Try to have fun," he told her.

"I'm getting there."

He gave her a thumbs-up.

They'd need some jewelry to go with it, of course. But that could be tomorrow's mission.

It occurred to Hunter that he was probably having a little too much fun at this himself. But he shrugged it off. Dressing a beautiful woman ought to be fun. And if a man couldn't have fun spending his money, what was the point in making any of it?

Jeanette herded Sinclair back into the change room, and Hunter returned to his phone call.

"Thanks for waiting," he said to Richard.

"Do you have a contact name?" asked Richard.

"Seth Vanderkemp. The Castlebay Spa headquarters is on Rue de Seline. Do we have a contract lawyer on standby?"

"We do. In fact, I can get someone there overnight. When will you know?"

"Tomorrow. If it looks like we can get a contract, I'll give you a call." Hunter knew this was their last chance to get Luscious Lavender into a spa chain in time for the Valentine's launch. If Castlebay was open to making a deal, he didn't want to lose a single minute.

He ended the call.

Immediately, his phone rang again.

"Hunter Osland."

"What the hell?" came his cousin Jack's voice.

"What the hell what?" asked Hunter, reflexively cataloguing his actions over the past couple of weeks to see what could have upset his cousin.

"One, you've got Sinclair in Paris? Two, there's trouble with her job. Three, you're dressing her like an android hooker. And four, you're probably sleeping with her? Take your pick."

"Oh, that," said Hunter.

"*That's* your answer?"

"What do you want me to say?" Hunter could tell his cousin to shut up and mind his own business. It was hardly a crime to go shopping. And he was behaving responsibly, particularly considering the attraction that still simmered between them.

"That you're not sleeping with my sister-in-law."

"I stopped."

"Good. Stay stopped. She works for us. And you're you."

"What the hell is that supposed to mean?"

"You know what it means."

Hunter sighed in exasperation. His reputation as a womanizer was not deserved.

"Tell Kristy I am not having a fling with her sister. Sinclair's job is not in jeopardy. And she doesn't look the least bit like a hooker."

"And you're not going to break her heart?"

Hunter pulled the phone away from his ear and frowned at it for a second. Then he put it back.

"Obviously, that was Kristy's question," Jack went on.

"What exactly have you told her about me?"

"Anything she asks. Plus, Gramps gave her the lowdown on some of your previous relationships. And you and Sinclair did start out with a one-night stand."

"Thanks for the support there, cousin."

Hunter hadn't had that many relationships. All right, some of them may have been short-lived. But they simply hadn't worked out. It wasn't as if he went around breaking hearts on purpose.

"Personally," said Jack, with more than a trace of amusement in his tone. "I'm more concerned about you. She's got red hair."

Hunter didn't bothering answering. He hit the end button and shoved the phone back in his pocket.

His cousin's joke was lame.

When Hunter was sixteen years old, he'd accidentally burned down the tent of an old gypsy fortune-teller. The woman had predicted Jack would marry a woman he didn't trust. They'd lose the family fortune. They'd buy a golf course. And Hunter would marry a redhead and have twins.

So far, the only thing that had come close to happening was Jack marrying Kristy before he trusted her. But it was enough to get Jack fixated on redheads and the possibility of twins.

The door to the changing room opened again.

Sinclair emerged in a strapless, jewel-blue, satin evening gown that revealed creamy cleavage on top and silver-strapped, sexy ankles on the bottom. She'd pinned her hair up in an ad hoc knot. As she moved gracefully toward him, the fabric rustled over her smooth calves, while her deep, coral lips curved into a satisfied smile.

Hunter's body reacted with a lurch, but then his stomach went hollow when he realized he couldn't touch her.

Kristy had absolutely nothing to worry about. If anybody was getting their heart broken around here, it sure wasn't going to be Sinclair.

Sinclair knew she'd be disappointed if Castlebay didn't work out. There was her job, her future, Hunter's reputation at the company, the success of the Luscious Lavender product line all to consider. And she'd reminded herself, she'd lived through two letdowns already. Still, walking up the stone steps to the Castlebay Spas head office, she was determined to fight the butterflies in her stomach.

"What should I focus on first?" she asked Hunter, anxious to get her part right.

She was wearing a mini, tweed coat dress, with pushed up sleeves, large black buttons, black stockings and high-heeled ankle boots. She'd pulled her hair into a simple, tight bob, as Jeanette had advised, and put on a little extra makeup, especially around the eyes.

"Leave the financial details to me. Give out product information only. If I brush your hand, stop talking. And, mostly importantly, walk, talk and act like a winner."

She gave him a swift nod.

"Oh. And mention that you've tried the mousse."

She shot him a disgusted stare.

"That was just to lighten you up." He pulled open the heavy brass and glass door. "Relax."

She took a breath. "Right."

They didn't talk in the elevator. And while they crossed the marble floor of the Castlebay lobby, Sinclair concentrated on her new shoes. She did not want to stumble.

"We have an appointment with Seth Vanderkemp," Hunter said to the receptionist.

Sinclair caught the woman's admiring look at her outfit, and she couldn't help but smile. Wouldn't the woman be surprised to find out she was staring at plain, old Sinclair Mahoney from Soho?

"Mr. Vanderkemp is expecting you," said the woman. "Right this way."

She stood and led them down a long hallway to an opulent meeting room. It had round beech-wood table, with a geometric, inlaid cherry pattern. There were four high-backed, burgundy leather chairs surrounding it. And the bank of windows overlooked the Seine.

"Good morning, Mr. Osland. Sorry to keep you waiting."

"Not at all," said Hunter. "We just got here. And, please, call me Hunter." He turned to Sinclair. "This is my associate, Sinclair Mahoney."

"Seth," said the man, holding out his hand to Sinclair. "Pleasure to meet you."

Sinclair shook. "Sinclair," she confirmed.

Seth gestured to the round table. "Shall we sit down?"

Hunter pulled out a chair for Sinclair, then the men sat.

"Osland International's latest acquisition," Hunter began, getting right to the point, "is a boutique beauty-products company out of New York called Lush Beauty."

"I've heard of Lush," said Seth with a nod.

Sinclair thought that fact boded well for the discussions, but Hunter's expression remained neutral.

"We're in Paris for a few days," explained Hunter, "looking for partners in the upcoming launch of a promising new line called Luscious Lavender."

Sinclair mentally prepared herself to talk about the products. She'd start with skin care, move to cosmetics, then introduce some of the specialty personal care items.

"With Osland International's involvement," Hunter continued, "we're in a position to launch simultaneously in North America and Europe. A spa would naturally be an ideal outlet for us, and we believe Castlebay's clientele are dead center for our target market."

Seth continued nodding, which Sinclair took to be a great sign.

"Under normal circumstances," he said, "I would agree with you. And I've no doubt that Luscious Lavender would serve our client market well. But, there's a complication."

Sinclair's stomach sank.

Hunter waited.

"There's an offer on the table to purchase Castlebay Spas in its entirety."

"What kind of an offer?" asked Hunter.

"I'm sure you realize I'm not in a position to discuss the particulars."

Hunter sat back in his chair. "Let me put it another way."

This time Seth waited.

So did Sinclair.

"What would it take to get the offer off the table?"

Seth looked puzzled. "In terms of…"

"In terms of another offer to purchase."

Seth's eyes narrowed. "Are you empowered—"

"I'm empowered."

Seth stood up, crossing to a telephone on a side table, and picked it up.

Sinclair stared at Hunter.

Seth asked, "Do you mind if the head of my legal department joins us?"

"Not at all," replied Hunter. "I assume you have a prospectus and some financials I could review?"

"It's all in order. Plus a full set of appraisals."

"Thank you," said Hunter.

Then he turned to Sinclair, he penned a few words on a business card he'd pulled from his pocket and handed it to her. "Could you call Richard Franklin? Have him set up a meeting at our hotel this afternoon. I'll meet you there."

Sinclair palmed the card and quietly left the room.

On the way across the lobby, heart pounding, mouth dry, she flipped over the card. On the back was Richard's name, his number and the phrase NO ONE ELSE.

Six

When Hunter reached the ground floor of the office building that housed Castlebay Spas, Sinclair was waiting on a bench near the exit.

She jumped to her feet as he neared. "I couldn't wait," she said.

"Apparently."

"If you came down with anyone else, I was going to hide."

Hunter couldn't help but grin.

"What happened?"

"Looks like we may be buying ourselves some spas."

Richard would have to review the contract, but Hunter was satisfied with the price. And, the combination of Lush Beauty and Castlebay Spas was going to be dynamite. His grandfather insisted Hunter run Lush Beauty Products? He was damn well going to run Lush Beauty Products.

"Just like that?" asked Sinclair, with a snap of her fingers.

"Just like that," echoed Hunter.

"I can't believe it." She skipped a step to keep pace with him. "So we can use Luscious Lavender in the spas?"

"That would be the point."

"How much—" She stopped. "Never mind." She shook her head. "None of my business."

"Lots," said Hunter. He'd drained the available cash in the Osland investment account, and put up a manufacturing plant as collateral to secure low ratio interest.

"How many spas?" she asked.

"Twelve. I have a list if you want it."

They started down the steps.

"You bet." Her face nearly burst with a grin. "So, what do we do now?"

"Who is Richard sending to the hotel?"

"Miles something…"

"We drop the papers off with Miles something for review. Then we carry on with your makeover."

"Do we celebrate?"

"As soon as the deal is approved," Hunter answered as they turned onto the sidewalk. "The financing has to be put in place first. And we need to get the signatures on the contracts."

She nodded eagerly.

"And, until then, we carry on as normal." He hesitated over the wording of the next part. "And we don't tell anyone about it."

She squinted up at him. "Anyone being?"

"Anyone. Including Kristy and Jack."

"But, why—"

"Convention." Hunter shrugged with feigned unconcern. "We investigate things like this all the time. No point in cluttering up everyone's desk over it until there's something concrete."

It wasn't exactly a lie, but it wasn't the whole truth, either. The deal was somewhat larger than Hunter would normally undertake on his own. And he hadn't yet figured out exactly how to tell Jack and his grandfather. He knew they'd be worried, and they'd definitely come at him with accusations that he was being reckless and impulsive. But he didn't have time for his grandfather's plodding approach to due diligence, which had taken weeks, even when he'd "rushed" the Lush deal.

Still, Hunter was fully confident in his decision. And he was fully confident time would prove it to be an excellent investment. But, for the short term, he needed a few days to work up to an explanation.

In the meantime, all the reasons for Sinclair's makeover remained.

"Jewelry store?" he asked her.

She laughed and unexpectedly captured his hand. "You *are* in a spending mood."

"I am," he agreed, kissing her knuckles and pointing to a five-story, stone-arched jewelry store across the street.

They dashed across the traffic and entered to discover the building decorated for Valentine's Day. Golden hearts, red ribbons and bows hung from the ceiling. Massive bouquets of red roses covered every surface. And tiny, heart-shaped boxes of truffles were being handed out to the ladies as they exited.

Hunter scanned the glass cases and the stairway leading to the second floor. Then he looked down at their clasped hands.

"You with me on this?" he asked.

She nodded.

He rubbed a finger across her nose. "No complaints now."

She took in the festive scene. "I'm not complaining."

"I may buy you something expensive."

"Just so long as you take it back when we're finished."

He frowned. "Take it back?"

"Save the box," she said. "Or you can give it to a girlfriend in the future."

Hunter had no intention of taking anything back, or giving it to some future girlfriend. But he didn't see any point in sharing that with Sinclair.

"Sure," he agreed.

Sinclair smiled and turned her attention to the display cases.

Convinced she was buying for some other mythical girlfriend—who Hunter could not remotely picture at the moment—Sinclair plunged right into the game.

She selected a sapphire-and-diamond choker, a pair of emerald-and-gold hooped earrings, teardrop diamonds, delicate sapphire studs, a ruby pendant that Hunter was positive she thought was an imitation stone, and a whimsical little bracelet with one ruby- and one diamond-encrusted goldfish dangling from the platinum chain.

Hunter bought them all, clipping the bracelet on her wrist so she could wear it back to the hotel.

Then they walked to a nice restaurant, taking seats overlooking the river. The maître d' brought them a bottle of merlot and some warm French rolls.

Sinclair jangled her bracelet. "You're very good at this."

"I have a mom and a sister."

"Nice answer," she nodded approvingly, lifting her long-stemmed glass. "Never buy for girlfriends?"

"Why do you keep setting me up?" He didn't want to talk to Sinclair about his former girlfriends. "Tossing out questions I can't answer without being a jerk?"

"I know you've had girlfriends."

"But I don't want to tell you about them."

"Why not? Wouldn't I like them?"

"You're really going to push this?"

"No reason not to."

"Is that what you're telling yourself?" He didn't know what was going on between them, but he sure as hell didn't want to hear about any of her old boyfriends.

Then again, maybe her feelings were different than his. There was one way to find out.

"Melissa," he said, watching Sinclair's expression carefully, "was a weather girl in Los Angeles. We dated for three months, played a lot of squash and beach volleyball. She was a vegetarian and a social activist. She wouldn't let me buy anything from a very long list of countries with human or animal rights infractions."

Sinclair's expression remained impassive.

Hunter tore one of the rolls in two. "Sandra worked in a health club. She also played squash. We dated maybe two months. Deanne taught parasailing. We did a lot of mountain climbing, and some swimming, and she loved dancing at the clubs. But I introduced her to one too many movie stars, and she was gone."

Sinclair's expression faltered. "Did she break your heart?"

Hunter scoffed out a laugh. "It was at the six-month mark, normally my limit. Now, Jacqueline—"

"Is this going to take the entire dinner?"

"You did ask."

"I've had two boyfriends," she offered.

"I *didn't* ask," Hunter reminded her.

"Roberto decided his mother was right after all, and Zeke drove off on his Harley."

They left her? Now, that surprised Hunter.

"They break your heart?" he found himself asking, genuinely wanting to know.

"I thought so at the time. But, you know, neither of them even took me to Paris."

Hunter grunted. "It's a sad day when a man won't even take his girlfriend to Paris."

"Now that I've seen Paris—" Sinclair spread her hands palms up "—that's going to be the baseline."

"Smart girl."

"Thank you."

"You might want to add diamonds to that list."

"You think?"

Hunter nodded and pretended to give it serious thought. "Private jet, too."

Sinclair picked up the other half of his roll. "How else does one get to Paris?" She took a bite.

"A woman needs to be smart about these things."

"Thank you so much for the advice."

To his surprise, Hunter wasn't jealous of Roberto and Zeke. The men were morons.

He signaled the waiter for menus, and sat back to enjoy the company.

Sinclair awoke with a smile on her face in the river-view room at the Ciel D'or Hotel in downtown Paris. She felt different. The clothes Hunter had bought her were hanging in the closet and the jewelry package was sitting on the nightstand. Someone was tapping gently on her door.

She flipped back the comforter and slipped into the plush, white hotel robe, tying the sash around her waist. The fish bracelet dangled at her wrist. She knew it was silly, but she hadn't wanted to take it off.

Through the peephole, she could see a black-tuniced waiter carrying a silver tray. Coffee. Her entire body sighed in anticipation.

She opened the door, and the man set the tray down on a small table beside the window. She realized she didn't have any money for a tip, but he assured her it was taken care of.

Before she had a chance to pour a cup of coffee or tear into one of the buttery croissants, the phone on the bedside table began to ring.

"Hello?" She perched on the edge of the unmade bed.

"You awake?" came Hunter's voice.

"Barely."

"Did the coffee arrive?"

"It did."

His breath hissed in. "Call me when you're dressed."

Her gaze darted to their connecting door. "I'm covered from head to toe."

"You sure?"

She glanced down. "Well, maybe not my toes. But everything else. Come and have coffee."

"Toes are sexy," he said in a rumbling voice.

"My nails need trimming, and I haven't had a pedicure in months."

"In that case, I'll be right over."

She grinned as she hung up the phone and opened her panel of the connecting door. Then she settled into one of the richly upholstered chairs and poured a cup of extremely fragrant coffee and gazed at the sparkling blue sky against the winter skyline.

The door on Hunter's side opened. "Did I mention the Castlebay Spa offers pedicures?"

"Are you offended by my toes?"

He took the seat across from her, pouring his own coffee.

"I'm not even going to look at your toes. If you lied about their condition, they'll probably haunt my dreams."

She tore a croissant in two. "You got a fetish?"

"Only for gorgeous women." His gaze caught her bracelet. Their eyes met, and there was something excruciatingly intimate in his look.

And then it hit Sinclair. They were having an affair. They were having an affair in every possible way except sleeping together. The awareness brought a warm glow to her stomach. She deliberately moved her hand so the bracelet would tap against her wrist. The sensation sent a shot of desire through her body.

Hunter cleared his throat. "So, do you want to continue the makeover in Paris, or perhaps we should switch our base of operations to London...or Venice?"

"Is there a better place than Paris for a brand-new hairdo?" She had absolutely no desire to leave.

"Not that I know of."

"Then I vote we stay here."

She sipped her coffee from the fine china cup and bit into the most tender croissant she'd had in her life.

Hunter selected an apple pastry sprinkled in powered sugar, and Sinclair decided she'd try that one next.

"Are you at all worried I'll get spoiled and refuse to go home?" she asked, taking another bite.

He grinned. "Go ahead."

"You're not serious."

He paused for a moment, gazing at her in the streaming sunlight. "Actually, I am. But you're not."

Sinclair didn't believe it for a second. Although it was nice of him to say so. As fantasies went, Hunter sure knew how to put on a good one.

"Have you called for a special opening of a hair salon?"

He shook his head. "I don't know anything about hair salons in Paris. But I do know people who know people."

"And they'll do you favors."

"They will."

"Why is that?"

"Because I'm a nice guy."

"That you are."

Sinclair sat back, gazing around the room, at the ornate moldings, the carved ceiling, the marble bathroom, and the four-poster bed. "But the money must be frustrating. I mean, how can you tell if people like you or not?"

He shrugged. "How does anybody tell? They're friendly. They don't jeer at me. They laugh at my jokes."

"But how can you tell it's you and not the money?"

"You can tell."

"I bet you can't."

"Most people are terrible liars."

Sinclair pushed her hair behind her ears. "Not me. I'm a great liar." She and Kristy had pulled the wool over her parents' eyes on numerous occasions.

"Yeah?" asked Hunter, his disbelief showing.

"Yeah," she affirmed with a decisive nod.

He put down the pastry and dusted the sugar off his hands with a nearby linen napkin. "Okay. Go ahead. Tell me a good lie."

Like she'd fall for that. "You'd already know it's a lie."

"Then tell me something that may or may not be a lie, and I'll tell you if it's the truth."

"Oh…kay." Sinclair thought about it. After a minute, she sat forward, warming to the game. "That morning at the Manchester mansion, I stole something from your room."

Hunter sat back in apparent surprise. "What did you steal?"

"Is it a lie or not?"

SAVE OVER £38 — 25% OFF

Sign up to get 4 books a month for 12 months in advance and **Save £38.28** – that's a fantastic 25% off
If you prefer you can sign up for 6 months in advance and **Save £15.31** – that's still an impressive 20% off

FULL PRICE	PER-PAID SUBSCRIPTION PRICE	SAVINGS	MONTHS
£153.12	£114.84	25%	12
£76.56	£61.25	20%	6

- Be the **FIRST** to receive the most up-to-date titles up to 2 months ahead of the shops
- Each book will cost **JUST £2.39** if you opt for a 12 month pre-paid subscription or £2.55 if you sign up for 6 months - the full price of each book would usually be £3.19

Plus to say thank you, we will send you a **FREE** L'Occitane gift set worth over £10

This offer is currently only available for new subscriptions to the Modern™ series. Gift set has a RRP of £10.50 and includes Verbena Shower Gel 75ml and Soap 110g

What's more you will receive ALL of these additional benefits

- Be the FIRST to receive the most up-to-date titles
- FREE P&P
- Lots of free gifts and exciting special offers
- Monthly exclusive newsletter

- Special REWARDS programme
- No Obligation –
  You can cancel your subscription at any time by writing to us at Mills & Boon Book Club, PO Box 676, Richmond, TW9 1WU.

P9K19

MILLS & BOON® Book Club

Sign up to save online at www.millsandboon.co.uk

He peered at her expression. "You're telling me you're a liar and a thief?"

She shook her head. "I'm either a liar *or* a thief. If I'm lying about being a thief, then I'm only a liar. But if I'm telling the truth about being a thief, I'm only a thief."

His eyes squinted down.

"Come on," she coaxed. "Which is it?"

"You're a liar," he said. "You didn't steal anything from my bedroom."

"You sure?"

"I'm positive."

"You got me," she admitted.

"Okay. Now it's my turn." He folded the napkin and set it aside. "I once wrestled an alligator."

"A real alligator?"

He nodded.

She was intrigued. Who wouldn't be? But she wasn't sold, yet. "Where?"

"A little town in Louisiana."

"Was it a trained alligator? Like in a zoo or something?"

"Nope. Out there in the bayou."

"It must have been pretty small."

"I didn't measure it or anything, but Jack guessed it was about six foot long."

"Jack was there, too?"

Hunter nodded.

Sinclair held out her hand. "Your phone."

"What?"

"I'm calling Jack."

"Oh, no, you're not."

"Oh, yes, I am." She wiggled her fingers.

Hunter shrugged and handed her the phone.

"You're *so* lying," she said. "Which speed dial?"

He grinned. "Four. And I'm not lying."

Sinclair hit number four, and waited while it rang. "You are busted," she said to Hunter.

"Jack Osland," came a sleepy voice. Too late, she remembered the time-zone difference.

"Hi, Jack," she offered guiltily. "It's Sinclair."

There was a pause. Jack's voice turned grave. "What did he do?"

She watched Hunter while she spoke. "He claims he wrestled a six-foot alligator in a Louisiana swamp."

"He told you that?"

"He did."

"Well, it's true."

Sinclair blinked. "Really?"

"Saved my life."

"Really?"

"Anything else?" asked Jack.

"Uh, no. Sorry. Bye." She shut off the phone. "You saved *his life.*"

Hunter shrugged. "He exaggerates."

Sinclair whooshed back in the chair. "I'd have bet money you were lying."

Hunter took a sip of his coffee. "I was."

She stilled. "What?"

He nodded "I was lying. I didn't wrestle a six-foot alligator. Are you kidding? I'd have been killed."

She looked down at the phone. "But…Jack…"

"Was lying, too."

"You couldn't possibly have set that up."

"We didn't have to." He lifted the phone from her hand. "You started the conversation by saying 'Hunter told me he wrestled an alligator.' Jack's my cousin; of course he's going to back me up."

"Tag-team lying?"

"It's the very best kind. Your turn."

"I'm not going to be able to top that."

"Give it a try."

Sinclair racked her brain. What could she possibly say that might throw him? Something believable, yet surprising.

Aha!

"I'm pregnant."

Hunter's face went white. "What?" he rasped.

Oh, no. No. She'd gone too far. "I'm lying, Hunter."

He worked his jaw, but no words came out.

"Hunter, seriously. I'm *lying.*"

"You're not pregnant?"

"I am not pregnant."

"If you were, would you tell me?"

"I'm not."

"Because we'd get married."

"Hunter. It's a game."

"Will you take a pregnancy test?"

"No."

"I let you phone Jack."

She stood up and rounded the table to him, bending over and putting all the sincerity she could muster into her eyes. "I'm sorry I said I was pregnant. I'm not."

He searched her expression. "You scared me half to death."

She smiled at that, reaching out to pat his cheek. "Not ready to be a daddy?"

He snagged her wrist and pulled her down into his lap. "Not ready for you to keep that big of a secret."

She shook her head. "I wouldn't. I'd tell you."

"Promise?"

"I promise."

He kissed the inside of her wrist. And then his gaze dipped down to her stomach.

She followed it and realized her movements had opened the robe. Her cleavage was showing, and the length of one thigh was visible nearly to her hip.

But Hunter wasn't looking at her thigh. His gaze was fixed on her stomach. His big, warm hand moved to press against the robe. It stayed there, and electricity vibrated between them. Then he slipped his hand beneath the robe to cup her soft stomach.

Arousal bloomed within her, radiating out to tingle her limbs. Her lips softened. Her eyelids went heavy. And she molded against his body.

He drew her head down, kissing her softly on the lips, trailing across her cheek, to the crook of her neck, to the tops of her breasts, burrowing down and inhaling deeply.

"I can't fight it anymore," he rasped, tipping to look up at her. "I can't."

"Then don't." She shook her head as she stared into the molten steel of his eyes. "Because it's killing us."

He bracketed her hips with his hands, lifting and turning her, so her legs went around his waist.

She ruffled her hands through his hair, kissing his hairline, his forehead, the tip of his nose.

He tugged the sash, and her robe fell away.

Then he smoothed his hands along her waist, wrapping around, splaying on her bare back, pulling her close over the rough fabric of his slacks. She bent her head and kissed his lips, slanting her mouth over his.

He met her tongue with his own, and she savored his taste,

content to let it last forever. But his hands slipped down, ratcheting up her arousal.

She whimpered.

"I know," he breathed, kissing her harder and deeper, letting his hands roam free, along her thighs, over her breasts, between her legs.

Her breathing turned labored, and she fought a war within herself. Part of her wanted him, right here, right now. Another part wanted to wait, to make it last. He felt good. He felt right.

She arched her back, pressing herself against his slacks.

He braced his forearms beneath her bottom, and came to his feet. She clung to his neck, anchoring her legs around his waist.

A few short steps, and they were there. The high four-poster. He set her down, then laid her back, pushing away the robe until she was completely naked.

She watched his hot gaze linger on her, not even considering adjusting her spread-legged pose. He traced a line between her breasts, down her belly, over her curls, into her center.

She closed her eyes, held on to the image of the unbridled arousal on his face.

She heard him stand.

Heard the rustle of his clothes.

The slide of his zipper.

The creak of his shoes.

"Sinclair?" he whispered, and she opened her eyes to see him standing naked above her.

She stretched out her hands, and he came down beside her, covering her with the weight of one thigh, smoothing her hair back from her face, kissing her gently on her cheek and on the tip of her shoulder.

"You are astonishingly, outrageously beautiful." His tone was reverent.

His words made her shiver.

He was beautiful, too. But more than that, he was Hunter. He was tender and funny, smart and determined—everything she could possibly dream of in a man.

"I want you so bad," he confessed.

Her throat closed up. She was beyond words, but she managed a nod of agreement.

"Do you remember?" he asked.

She nodded again, finding her voice. "Everything," she rasped. *"Everything."*

He inched a hand up her ribcage, finding the soft underside of her breast. He smoothed his thumb over the peak, drawing a lazy circle, pulling her nipple to a pebble. "I remember it, too."

Then he proved his knowledge, finding secrets and hollows, making her purr and moan.

She reached for him in return, running her fingertips over his chest and abdomen. He sucked in a breath as she brushed his erection. He let her test the length and texture, before trapping her wrist and calling a halt.

He pushed her arms over her head, where they had to behave. Then he kissed her mouth, and her neck, and her breasts. He released her hands, as his lips roamed free, testing and suckling. She tangled his hair, moaning his name, everything inside her tightening and heightening.

But he kissed his way back. And merged with her mouth. He moved atop her, linking his fingertips with hers, pressing them down against the softness of the comforter. Her knees moved apart, and their bodies met, slick and hot and impossibly sweet.

He eased inside her, slower than she could bear. She thrashed her head and squeezed his hands, her kisses growing deeper and more frantic. Then she instinctively flexed her hips, and he pushed the final inch to paradise.

He set a rhythm, speeding up and slowing down. She felt the fire of passion build within her. Her eyes squeezed shut, and her focus contracted to the spot where their bodies met.

The world turned to heat, and sensation and scent. She felt his muscles clench, and his desire take over. He sped up and stayed there, his thrusts intent and solid. A moan started low in her throat. It grew louder and more frantic, until she cried out his name, and the world fell apart, and his body pulsed within her.

They breathed in sync for long minutes after.

"You okay?" His voice seemed to come from a long way off. His body was a delicious weight on top of her, and she couldn't move a muscle, including her eyelids.

"Sinclair?" he pressed, sounding worried.

"I think we've cured the tension," she mumbled.

There was a chuckle low in his throat, and he eased his weight to the side, gathering her in his arms. "I do believe you're right."

Seven

Sinclair caught sight of her new haircut in the mirror at Club Seventy-Five. She'd second-guessed herself about getting it so short, but she had to admit, she loved it. Textured to spiky wisps around her ears and neck, it was light on top, and her new bangs swooped across her forehead, while the foil, blond highlights brought out the color in her cheeks.

Of course, the color could have come from the tote bag full of Luscious Lavender cosmetics that she'd had applied this afternoon. The beautician had painstakingly shown Sinclair how to apply the makeup herself, but she wasn't so sure she'd be successful—at least not without a lot of practice.

But, for tonight, she felt gorgeous.

She was wearing one of the jazzier dresses they'd bought at La Petite Fleur. A Diana Kamshak, it was a mint-green satin party dress. The short, full skirt sported blue horizontal stripes, and it was accented by a blue and silver border at the mid-thigh hem.

Above the wide silver belt, the top was tight and strapless, with a princess neckline that drew attention to her breasts. She wouldn't normally be comfortable in something so revealing. But every time she looked into Hunter's eyes, she felt beautiful.

She'd had dozens of covetous looks at her sapphire-and-diamond choker. Or perhaps it was because she was also wearing the Diana Kamshak dress. Or perhaps it was because she was with Hunter.

She'd decided on the teardrop diamond earrings, and she liked the way their weight bounced on her ears. She still hadn't taken off the goldfish bracelet, and it made a kicky addition to the outfit. She liked it. She liked it all.

The lights and the music pounded lifeblood through her bones. Or maybe it was Hunter that pounded through her bones. They were out on the floor, amidst the crowd, alternating between touching, smiling, and just moving independently to the beat.

He slipped an arm around her waist, tugging her close, spinning her to the rhythm of the house band. Sinclair smiled, then laughed out loud, she couldn't help it. The musicians launched into another lively and compelling tune.

"You thirsty?" he called in her ear as the song finished with a metallic flourish.

She nodded.

He put at hand at the small of her back, guiding her off the dance floor. "Water? Wine? Champagne?"

Sinclair did a little shimmy next to their table. "Champagne."

He gave her a kiss on the cheek. "My kind of girl."

Then he helped her into the high bar chair and disappeared into the crowd.

Sinclair liked being Hunter's kind of girl.

She liked the fashions. She liked the limos. She loved the sex. And she loved the way they arrived at a club and got escorted immediately through the side entrance. No waiting around on the curb for Hunter Osland.

But putting all that aside, what she liked most of all was Hunter—the person. Period.

Okay, the one thing she didn't like was the high shoes. She supposed she'd get used to them at some point, but right now, they just made one of her baby toes burn and both calves ache.

She slipped the heels off under the table.

Hunter returned with the drinks as the band announced a break. She sipped at the bubbles and grinned.

"Good?" asked Hunter, picking up his own glass.

"Great," said Sinclair.

Two men slid into the other chairs at the table. "Hey, Osland," one greeted.

"Bobby," said Hunter. "Nice to see you." Then he nodded to the other man. "Scooter."

Scooter nodded back.

Then both men smiled appreciatively at Sinclair.

"Sinclair Mahoney," Hunter introduced. "This is Bobby Bonnista and Scooter Hinze from Blast On Black."

"Sorry," said Sinclair, leaning into Hunter's shoulder. "I should have recognized you right away but I guess I was focused on Hunter."

Hunter's chest puffed out, and he put an arm around her. "What can I say?"

Both men guffawed at his posturing, but smiled at Sinclair and held out their hands.

She shook. "Loved the music."

"Thanks," Bobby nodded. "We're trying out some new stuff tonight. It's always a challenge."

"Well, it's great," she said sincerely.

"Got time for a drink?" asked Hunter.

Bobby shook his head. "We're on in ten minutes."

A server stopped at the table and topped up Sinclair's glass of champagne.

The two musicians rose from their chairs. "Coming to the party?" asked Bobby. "Suite 1202 at the Ivy."

"Not sure," said Hunter.

The men glanced at Sinclair with a sly, knowing grin. But, surprisingly, Sinclair found she didn't mind.

"Sorry about that," said Hunter after they'd left.

She shrugged. "Were they wrong?"

He leaned very close to her ear. "That," he rumbled, "is entirely up to you."

Blast On Black took the stage once more.

Sinclair wriggled her feet back into the strappy sandals. "Want to dance?"

Sinclair's shoes dangled from her fingertips as they made their way down the hotel hallway.

"Tired?" asked Hunter, slipping the key card into her room lock.

"A little tipsy," she admitted, crossing the threshold and tossing her shoes in the corner. The bed had been turned down and the adjoining door left open.

"Champagne in France will do that to you."

"It was delicious." She took a deep breath and blinked away the buzzing in her head.

Hunter locked the door, then reached into his pocket to retrieve his cell phone. He pressed the on button and sighed.

"Messages?" she asked, digging into her purse to check her own phone.

"Thirty-five," he said, hitting the scroll button with his thumb.

"I have six," she frowned. "Boy, do I feel unpopular." Two of them were from Kristy, the rest from the office. She'd been keeping in touch with Amber via e-mail, making sure the ball plans were under control, despite Chantal's meddling.

"Enjoy it," he advised. Then he pressed a couple of keys, putting the phone to his ear.

"Hey, Richard," he said.

Then he waited in silence.

Sinclair struggled to reach the zipper on her dress.

"They did?" said Hunter.

She gave up and crossed the room to Hunter, turning her back. She automatically reached to pull her hair out of the way, but it wasn't there. She touched the top of her head, raking her fingers through her new short hair, enjoying the light feel while Hunter tugged down her zipper.

She wandered into the bathroom to find fresh towels and robes. Stepping out of her dress, she shrugged into a robe. She scrubbed off her makeup and carried the dress to the closet. She'd have to send it for cleaning tomorrow, but she didn't have the heart to toss it on a chair overnight. It was a fabulous dress.

"Thanks, Richard," Hunter was saying. "That's great news."

The tone of his voice caught Sinclair's attention.

Hunter snapped his phone shut. "It's done."

"What's done?"

"You are looking at the new owner of Castlebay Spas. Everything should clear escrow tomorrow."

A huge grin burst out on Sinclair's face. "That's fantastic!" She skipped across the room to give him a hug.

He nodded against her shoulder, squeezing her tight.

"Sweetheart, the two of us are going to launch Lush Beauty to the stars."

"As long as I can keep up the glam charade so Roger is happy."

"I'll fire Chantal tomorrow if that's what it takes."

Sinclair sobered. "You wouldn't do that, would you?"

"I won't have to."

"But, even if you did. You'd never do that. I mean, I couldn't live with myself if I built a career based on your intervention."

He took both her hands in his and squeezed. "It'll never happen. Seriously. Stop borrowing trouble. We just had some amazingly good news, and we need to celebrate. And we need to plan a tour of the spas. Rome, London…"

She felt better. The makeover was moving along as planned, and the spa launch was more than she'd ever dreamed.

He loosened the knot in his tie. "I'm going next door to shower."

"Okay."

"While I'm gone, you get happy again. Okay?"

"I will."

"Good." He winked at her, stripping off the tie as he strode through the adjoining door.

Sinclair curled up in an armchair. She mentally did the math on time zones and realized she could safely return Kristy's calls.

"Hello," came Kristy's voice.

"Hey, it's me."

"*You*. Finally! What the heck's going on?"

"I'm still in Paris."

"Wonderful, dear sister. But tell me how you ended up in Paris in the first place?"

"We took the jet. That's one very cool jet, by the way."

"Funny. What on earth happened at work?"

"You remember my boss, Roger?"

"Short guy, big nose."

"That's him. Well, he's got this new protégée, Chantal, who's off the charts avante garde, giggly and girly and squealy. And he's decided she's the face Lush Beauty needs for PR."

"They fired you?"

"No. Nobody fired me. But I can easily see her at the podium and me in a dingy back file room if things keep going like this."

"You know Hunter's the CEO now, right?" asked Kristy.

"And, so?"

"Well, you are my sister…."

Sinclair was slightly insulted. "You're suggesting nepotism?" That was as bad as sleeping her way to the top.

"You don't need nepotism. But if Roger and this Chantal are out to lunch—"

"Actually, Hunter agrees with them."

Silence.

"He thinks my image could use some updating."

Kristy's voice took on an incredulous quality. "And you're okay with that? That doesn't sound like you."

Sinclair had to agree that it didn't sound like her. And she'd been avoiding delving too closely into her motivations for going along with him.

"True. But the new wardrobe is nice."

Concern grew in Kristy's voice. "Sinclair, you're not—"

"I'm not."

"—falling for Hunter. Because I've been talking to Jack, and to his grandfather, and he's not a good long-term prospect."

"You're getting ahead of yourself," said Sinclair, embarrassed that Kristy would have discussed the situation with the Osland family.

"You remember how you were after Zeke."

"I got over Zeke just fine." It hadn't taken that long, maybe a few weeks. "And I have Hunter completely in context."

"You sure?"

"I'm sure." Well, kind of sure. "It's all business," Sinclair insisted. "In fact, we're about to launch Lush Beauty in the biggest way." She thought about the spa deal and the time spent with Hunter. "Do you ever find your new life with Jack surreal?"

Kristy laughed. "All the time."

"Hunter and I went to a club tonight. First class all the way. The band even stopped by. And the weird thing? It seemed pretty normal."

"It does take some getting used to," Kristy agreed.

"Yeah, for the launch of the new Luscious Lavender line across Europe, Hunter bought a chain of spas!" She heard him moving around next door. "Sounds like he's out of the shower."

"Hunter is in your *shower?* What the—"

"He's next door. We have adjoining rooms." Then Sinclair realized she probably didn't want to have a detailed conversation on that, particularly when Hunter was about to waltz back into her room. "Better go."

"Wait—"

"Bye." Sinclair quickly disconnected.

"Hey, babe," said Hunter, padding inside in one of the white robes. "You're not going to shower?"

She stifled a yawn, dropping her phone on the little desk beside the armchair. "Tomorrow."

He crossed toward her. "Works for me." He smiled as he leaned down to kiss her. "Ready for bed?"

"Just let me find something to change into."

He burrowed into her neck, planting kisses along the way. "You're not going to need a nightgown."

She chuckled at his gravelly voice and the way his rough skin tickled hers.

His hands slipped beneath her robe. "What's this?"

"It's called underwear."

"You trying to slow me down?"

"Not worth the work, am I?"

"Always." He drew her to her feet.

Then his cell phone rang.

He swore, but picked it up and checked the number. "Richard."

"You need to take that?"

"Tomorrow," he said. "Tomorrow, we need to strategize."

"Over the spas?"

He nodded.

Sinclair squinted. "I thought the deal was done?"

"It is." His lips compressed. "Tomorrow I figure out how to explain to my family I spent several hundred million."

Everything inside Sinclair went still. "How do you mean?"

"I mean, I'm going to hear words like *reckless* and *impulsive.* They'll be ticked, so I need to figure out how to present this just right so Gramps doesn't go ballistic."

Her stomach turned to a lead weight. "But I thought…"

He waited.

"I thought you were ready to tell them."

He coughed out a cold laugh. "Not hardly." He tossed the phone down and moved toward her. "But it can wait until tomorrow; you're what's important tonight."

"I have to use the bathroom," Sinclair blurted.

"Sure," he said, obviously puzzled as to why she was

making a big deal about it. "You should go ahead and do that."

Hesitating only a second, she grabbed her phone.

He glanced at her hand. "Expecting a call?"

"Maybe. I don't know." She headed for the door. "Time zones, you know." Then she quickly shut herself in.

Her hands were shaking as she dialed Kristy.

"Come on. Come on," she muttered as the connection rang hollow. "Pick up."

She got her sister's voice mail and jiggled her foot as she waited for the beep.

"Kristy? It's me. I *really* need to talk to you. I'll try again in a few minutes. Make sure you pick up."

What to do now? She needed Hunter out of the way. She needed Hunter…asleep.

Okay, this was going to be tricky. He didn't seem like he was in the mood for anything remotely quick.

She exited the bathroom, and was pulled immediately into his arms, engulfed in a major hug, peppered with kisses that under any other circumstances would have been erotic and totally arousing.

"Uh, Hunter?"

"Yeah?"

"I'm…not…"

He pulled back. "Something wrong?"

"I'm still woozy from the drinks," she lied.

His eyes glowed pewter as he waggled his eyebrows. "You maybe need to lie down?"

She shook her head. "No. I mean yes. I mean." She hit him with the most contrite expression she could muster. "Can we wait until morning?"

His gaze grew concerned. "That bad?"

She nodded. It was worse, only not in the way he was imagining.

"Come on, then." He led her to the bed, pushing aside the comforter and tucking her in.

He slipped under the covers beside her and spooned their bodies together. He kissed the back of her neck, smoothing her hair. "Sleep," he muttered.

She nodded miserably, and pretended to do just that.

Half an hour later, his breathing was deep and even. Engulfed in his warmth, she was struggling to stay awake herself. She didn't dare wait any longer.

She cautiously slipped from the bed, snagged her phone, and tiptoed into the bathroom.

She tried Kristy again, still coming up with voice mail.

"Kristy?" she whispered harshly. "You have to call me. I'm sleeping with my phone on vibrate. Wake me up!"

Then she clicked it off, forced herself to swallow her panic, took a drink of water to combat her dry throat, and headed back to bed.

"You okay?" Hunter mumbled as she climbed back in.

"Thirsty," she responded guiltily as he drew her against him.

"You'll be better in the morning," he assured her with a kiss.

She'd be better when Kristy called and was sworn to temporary secrecy. That's when she'd be better.

Sinclair awoke to Hunter's broad hand on her breast. His lips were kissing her neck, and his hardened body was pressed against her backside.

"Morning, sweetheart," he murmured in her ear.

She smiled. "Morning."

He caressed her nipple, sending sparks of desire to her

brain. His free hand trailed along her belly. She gasped, the warmth of arousal swirling and gathering within her.

"I've been waiting," he rumbled. "You slept too long."

"Sorry."

"Make it up to me." His hand slipped to the moisture between her legs.

He flipped her onto her back.

"Right now," he growled.

In answer, she kissed him hard.

A pounding sounded on the door, and someone shouted his name.

Hunter jerked back. "What the—?"

It took her a second to realize the person was pounding outside Hunter's room.

"Don't move," he commanded, staring into her eyes. Then he jackknifed out of bed and stuffed his arms into the robe. He pushed the adjoining door shut behind him. Sinclair sat up, shaking out the cobwebs.

She felt a lump under her thigh, and realized it was her phone. Flipping it open, she quickly checked for a return call from Kristy.

Nothing.

The voices rose in the room next door, drawing Sinclair's attention.

"—be so freaking reckless and impulsive!"

It was Jack's voice, and Sinclair was afraid she might throw up.

"We have talked and *talked* about this," came another gravelly voice. It had to be Cleveland.

The family knew. They were here. And they were angry. And it was all her fault. Sinclair wrapped her arms around her stomach and scrunched her eyes shut tight.

* * *

At first, Hunter was too shocked to react.

He'd gone from Sinclair, soft and plaint in his arms, to his grandfather's harsh wrath in the space of thirty seconds. His brain and his hormones needed time to catch up.

"I can give you the prospectus," he told them. "The financials and the appraisals."

"You can bet your ass you'll be giving us the prospectus, the financials and the appraisals," shouted Gramps.

Then it was Jack's turn. "You can't make unilateral decisions!"

"I can. And so can you and Gramps."

"Not like this."

"Yes, like this. There's no advantage in three guys spending time on what one can do alone." Hunter was warming up now. He just wished he was wearing something other than a bathrobe. "This is a good deal. It's a *great* deal!"

"That's not the point," Jack said.

"The point being that you and Gramps are control freaks?"

"The point being you need to play with the team."

Hunter turned on his grandfather. "You thought it was funny to send me to Lush Beauty. You thought it was funny to send me to Sinclair. Well, guess what? You send me to run a company, I run the damn company."

"I have half a mind to take away your signing authority," Cleveland threatened.

"Because that wouldn't be an overreaction," Hunter countered, folding his arms across his chest.

"You, young man, spent hundreds of millions without so much an e-mail."

"It's amortized over twenty years. The property values alone—"

"If it wasn't for Sinclair telling Kristy—"

"What?" Hunter roared, unable to believe what he'd heard. Jack and Cleveland stopped dead.

Hunter stared hard at them. "You got information from your wife because my…Sinclair talked?"

"And thank God she did," said Cleveland.

But Hunter was past listening to Jack and his grandfather.

"We're done," he said to them, moving to open the door. "Richard has the details. You take a look at the deal. If you don't like it, I'll sell my Osland International stock and go it on my own."

Jack squinted. "Hunter?"

Hunter swung open the hotel room door. "Talk to you later."

"It wasn't Sinclair's—"

"Talk to you later."

Jack moved in front of him. "I can't let you—"

"What?" Hunter barked. "What do you think I'm going to do to her?"

"I don't know."

"Give me a break," he scoffed. He wasn't going to hurt Sinclair. He wouldn't let anybody hurt Sinclair. But the woman had one hell of a lot of explaining to do.

Eight

Hearing the latch click on the adjoining door, Sinclair broke out in a cold sweat. Her fingertips dug into the arms of the chair as she stared straight at the dove-gray painted panel.

The hinges glided silently and Hunter filled the doorway, his eyes simmering obsidian. But his voice was cool with control. "I thought we were a team."

She wished he'd shout at her, wished he'd rant. She could take his anger a lot more easily than his disappointment.

She'd let him down. She wanted to explain. She wanted to apologize. But her vocal cords were temporarily paralyzed.

"I trusted you," he continued. "I trusted your confidentiality. I trusted your discretion."

She fought to say something, to gather her thoughts. "I didn't know," she finally blurted out.

"Didn't know what? Was there something ambiguous about 'don't tell anyone, including Kristy and Jack'?"

"But that was before the deal went through."

"The deal went through at 3:00 a.m. this morning. Are you telling me in the five minutes I was in the shower—" He snapped his jaw. "You called Kristy." He gave a cold laugh. "You were so anxious to share gossip about my business dealings that you couldn't even wait until morning?"

"It wasn't gossip."

"Do you have any idea what you've done?"

She slowly shook her head. She could only imagine the implications of her behavior now that she had all the facts.

"Well, that makes two of us," he said. "Because I just offered to sell out of Osland International."

The contents of her stomach turned to a concrete mass.

She opened her mouth, but he waved a dismissive hand. "Much as I'd like to sit around and debate this with you, I've got a few problems to solve this morning. I'll have to talk to you later."

Then he turned back to his own room, shutting the door firmly behind him.

Sinclair's cell phone chimed.

She glanced reflexively down to see Kristy's number on the readout. She couldn't talk to her sister now. She didn't think she could talk to anyone.

There was every possibility she'd ruined Hunter's life. The worry that she might not get plum assignments or choice promotions at Lush Beauty faded to nothing in the face of that reality.

She stared at nothing for nearly an hour, then shoved herself into a standing position. She crossed to the closet and took out the clothes she'd been wearing when she arrived in Paris. They looked pale and boring compared to the new outfits, but she didn't have the heart to wear any of them.

She combed her hair, brushed her teeth, left the cosmetics on the counter and gathered up the suitcase with her old clothes inside. It seemed like a long walk to the elevator, longer still across the marble-floored atrium in the hotel lobby.

She figured Hunter would check out for her, so she wound her way past smiling tourists, bustling bellboys and intense businessmen. The men reminded her of Hunter and made her sadder by the moment.

Finally, she was out on the sidewalk, glancing up and down for a taxi. A hotel bellhop asked her a question in French. She tried to remember how to ask for a taxi, but it had slipped her mind.

In the sidewalk café next to her, propane heaters chugged out the only warmth in her world. People were eating breakfast, enjoying the sights of the busy street, their lives still intact.

The bellhop asked the question again.

She remembered. "Cabine de taxi?"

"Going somewhere?" came Hunter's voice from behind her.

"The airport," she answered without turning.

"I thought Mahoneys didn't run away."

"I'm not running away."

"You mad at me?"

The question surprised a cold laugh from her.

"Because I'm pretty mad at you," he said.

"No kidding."

A taxi pulled up, but Hunter let someone else take it. "So, what's your plan?"

She sighed. "Why'd you do that?"

"We're not finished talking."

"I thought you had problems to solve."

He snorted. "And how. But I want to know your plans first."

Sinclair looked pointedly down at her suitcase.

"You left the rest of your clothes in the closet," he said.

"Those are your clothes."

"So, you're going to pout? That's your plan?"

"I'm not pouting." She was making a strategic exit from an untenable situation before he had a chance to ask her to go himself.

Another taxi came to a stop, and Hunter sent it away.

"Do you think we could sit down?" he asked with a frustrated sigh, gesturing to the café.

Sinclair shrugged. If he wanted to ream her out some more, she supposed she owed him that much.

He picked up her suitcase, and she moved to one of the rattan chairs. She folded her hands on the round glass table and looked him straight in the eyes.

"Go ahead," she said, steeling herself.

"You think I'm here to yell at you?"

She didn't answer.

"Good grief, you're as bad as Jack." Hunter signaled the waitress for coffee, and Sinclair decided it might be a very long lecture.

"It seems to me…" said Hunter, as the uniformed woman filled their cups. He shook out a packet of sugar, tore off the corner and dumped it into the mug.

Sinclair just stared at the rising steam.

"You have two choices," Hunter continued. "You can slink back to New York with your makeover half done and take your chances with Roger. Or you can buck up and stay here a few more days to finish it."

"It seems to me," she offered, forcing him to get to the heart of the matter. "Those are your choices, not mine."

"How so?"

"Why would you want me to stay? Why would you want to help me? I ruined your life."

"We don't know that yet."

"Well, I might have."

"Possibly. Did you do it on purpose?"

"Of course not."

"So you weren't dishonest, you simply lacked certain details and a little good judgment."

She tightened her jaw. She normally had great judgment. "Right," she said.

A small glimmer flickered in his eyes. "You want to fight me, don't you?"

She wrapped her hands around the warm stoneware mug. "I'm in the wrong. I can take it."

"Very magnanimous of you."

"Are we done? Can I go now?"

"Do you want to go now?"

She didn't answer.

"Seriously, Sinclair. Do you want to walk out on Paris, the makeover and me just because things went off the rails?"

Things had done a lot more than go off the rails. She forced herself to ask him, "What do you want?"

"I want to turn the clock back a couple of hours to when you were sleeping in my arms."

"I want to turn it back nine."

He nodded, and they sat in silence for a few moments while dishes clattered and voices rose and fell at nearby tables. A gust of cool wind blew through, while the propane heaters chugged gamely on.

Hunter took a sip of his coffee. "Let me tell you why Jack and Gramps were so upset."

"Because you spent hundreds of millions of dollars without

telling them?" As soon as the flip answer was out, she regretted it. "Sorry."

But Hunter actually smiled. "Good guess. It's because they wanted me to call them first. They wanted to jump in and assess the deal before I made a decision. They wanted to research and analyze and contemplate. Do you have any idea how long Jack and Cleveland's brand of due diligence takes?"

Sinclair shook her head.

"The deal would have been lost before they even lined up the legal team."

"Did you explain that to them?"

He shot her a look. "That was my plan. Until you stepped in."

"Sorry," she said again, knowing it would never be enough.

"I know you are." But he didn't sound angry. He sounded resigned.

Cars whizzed by on the narrow street, while a contingent of Japanese businessmen amassed on the sidewalk nearby.

"What will you do now?" Sinclair asked.

"That's entirely up to you."

"You're seriously willing to keep this up?"

He nodded. "I am. There may be a lot of yelling from Jack and Gramps over the next few days, but I want to finish what we started."

"I can handle yelling."

"Good. You know anything about ballroom dancing?"

"Not much."

"Then that's next on our list." His expression softened. "You are going to take their breath away."

A knot let go in Sinclair's stomach.

"Flower for the pretty lady?" came an old woman's gravelly voice. She held a white rose toward Hunter, her bangles and hoop earrings sparkling against colorful clothing and a bright silk headscarf. "I will tell her fortune."

Hunter accepted the flower and nodded.

The old woman clasped Sinclair's hands, her jet-black eyes searching Sinclair's face. Then she smiled. "Ahhh. Fertility."

"I'm going to be a farmer?"

The woman revealed a snaggle-toothed smile, her gaze going to Sinclair's stomach.

Sinclair sure didn't like the implication of that.

"Trust your heart," said the old woman.

"I'm not pregnant," Sinclair pointed out.

The old woman released Sinclair's hands and touched her chin. "I see wealth and beauty."

"That's a whole lot better than fertility," Sinclair muttered.

Hunter laughed and reached for his wallet.

Sinclair caught the numbers on the bills he passed to the woman. Both hers and the old woman's eyes went wide.

The woman quickly hustled away.

"Did you know her or something?" Sinclair asked.

"I once knew somebody like her." Hunter tucked his wallet into his pocket and handed Sinclair the rose.

She held it to her nose and inhaled the sweet fragrance. Hunter wanted her to stay. The relief nearly brought tears to her eyes.

"Somebody like her?" she asked Hunter, inhaling one more time. "I once burned down a gypsy's tent." Then he smiled gently at Sinclair.

He swiveled his coffee mug so the handle was facing him. "When I was a teenager, a gypsy at the local circus told my fortune. She said I'd fall for a redheaded girl and have twins."

Sinclair reflexively touched her hair.

"The thought of twins freaked me out, too. I wanted to be a rock star."

"So, you burned down her tent?"

"She also said Jack would marry a woman he didn't trust, and we'd buy a golf course."

"But, you burned down her tent?" Sinclair repeated.

"It was an accident."

"You sure?"

He rocked back. "Hey, is there anything about me that strikes you as vindictive?"

"I guess not," she admitted, a small smile forming on her lips. Heck, he wasn't even kicking her out for ruining his life.

"It was an accident. And Gramps compensated her fairly. But, I guess I've always felt a little guilty."

"Have you been giving money to random gypsies ever since?"

"It's not like I come across a lot of them. Alhough…" He pretended to ponder. "I suppose a charitable foundation wouldn't be out of order."

"I'm sure they appreciate it."

Sinclair's cell phone chimed.

She opened her purse to check the lighted number. "Kristy."

It chimed again under her hand.

"Better answer it," Hunter advised. "She's probably worried."

"So was I," Sinclair said over the sound.

His hand covered hers for a brief second. "We'll talk more."

Sinclair pressed a button and raised the phone to her ear. "Hey, Kristy."

"You okay?"

"Yeah. I'm fine."

"And Hunter?"

Sinclair looked at him. "He's had better mornings."

"What was he *thinking?*" There was a clear rebuke in

Kristy's tone. "Going out on his own. Jack says that Hunter was being dangerously cavalier with the family fortune."

Some protective instinct leapt to life within Sinclair. "He was thinking it was a good deal."

Hunter shook his head, mouthing the word, "Don't."

Sinclair ignored him. "And they might want to look closely at it before they decide it's a bad risk."

Hunter stood to lean over the table, but Sinclair turned away, protecting the phone. The least she could do was come down on his side.

"Are you *defending* him? Did he try to make this your fault? It wasn't your fault, you know. You were being honest. He was being underhanded."

"He was being smart."

There was a shocked silence on the line.

"Are you sleeping with him again?" Kristy demanded.

"None of your business."

"That's it. I'm coming to Paris."

Hunter lunged forward and grabbed the phone from Sinclair's hands.

"Goodbye," she quickly called as he snapped it shut.

"Have you lost your mind?" asked Hunter.

"She said you were being underhanded."

"You can't fight with your sister over me."

Sinclair folded her arms over her chest and blew out a breath. "Sure, I can."

Hunter handed back the phone. "No. You can't. She's your sister. Keep your eye on the long game."

Meaning Hunter was the short game?

"And she loves you," he said.

"She's coming to Paris."

"You want to go to London?"

Sinclair grinned. "We couldn't."

Hunter sighed. "You're right. We couldn't."

She caught a figure in her peripheral vision, turning to see Jack pulling up a chair at their table.

"You okay?" he asked Sinclair.

"You're as bad as Kristy," Sinclair responded. "What exactly do you think he'd do to me?"

"What *did* he do?"

"He invited me to go ballroom dancing. We're getting ready for the Valentine's Day ball on Thursday."

Jack shot his gaze to Hunter. "That true?"

"What if it is?"

"I just had a call from Kristy," said Jack.

"She's coming to Paris," announced Sinclair.

Jack nodded. "That's what she said." He was still eyeing up Hunter suspiciously. "You'd better sign us up, too."

After the day they'd had, Hunter wanted nothing more than to curl up in bed and hold Sinclair tight in his arms. He'd discovered he hated fighting with her. And he hated that her family and his had decided to protect her from him. Even now, across the floor in the Versailles Ballroom, Kristy was scoping them out, staring daggers at him.

A private jet had whisked her across the Atlantic in time for dinner.

Part of him wanted to thumb his nose at the lot and haul Sinclair away so they could be alone. Another part of him recognized they had legitimate concerns. His efforts to help her had gotten all mixed up with his desire for her.

He didn't want to hurt her, but he might in the end. The Lush Valentine's Day ball was only a few days away. He'd make sure she was a smash hit there, but then what?

She'd still work for him. Could they possibly keep sleeping together? Could they keep it a secret? And what did that say about them if they did?

As he guided her through a simple waltz, he considered the possibility that Kristy was right. After all, who would have Sinclair's best interests at heart more than her twin sister? A twin sister whose thinking wasn't clouded by passion?

God knew his was clouded by something.

Sinclair had dressed for the evening in a brilliant-red strapless satin gown. When he glanced at her creamy shoulders, the hint of cleavage, and her long, smooth neck, his thoughts were definitely on his own best interest. And that best interest was in peeling the gown off inch by glorious inch to reveal whatever it was she had, or didn't have, on underneath.

The bodice molded gently over her breasts, it nipped in at her waist, then molded over her bottom, while the full skirt whispered around her gorgeous legs.

"How am I doing?" she asked as the music's tempo changed.

"Fine," he told her, forcing his thoughts back to his job as dance instructor. "Ready to try something more?"

She nodded, blue eyes shining up at him, making him wish all over again that he could whisk her away.

He led her into a turn. She stumbled, but he held her up, tightening his hand in the small of her back, filing the sensation away in his brain.

"Sorry," she told him.

"No problem. Just pay attention to my hand," he reminded her, demonstrating the touches. "This means left. This means right. Back, and forward."

He tried the turn again.

She stumbled.

He tried one more time, and this time she succeeded.

But, while she grinned, she fumbled the next step.

He tried not to smile at her efforts. "I can see this is going to take practice."

"You're too sudden with your signals. And why do you get to call all the moves?"

"Because I'm the man."

"That's lame."

"And because I know how to dance."

"Okay, that's better."

Someone tapped Hunter on the shoulder. He turned to see Jack, looking to switch partners. Before he knew it, Kristy was in his arms.

"Hello, Hunter." She smiled, but he could see the glitter of determination behind her eyes.

"Hello, Kristy."

"I see you've spirited my sister away to Paris."

"I'm helping her out."

"That's one way to put it."

"What's another?" he challenged, keeping half an eye on Jack and Sinclair.

"Why don't you tell me what your intentions are?"

To have sex with Sinclair—the most amazing woman I've ever met—until we can't see straight. "I don't know what you mean?" he stalled.

"You know exactly what I mean."

He did. And that was the problem. His interests and Sinclair's did not coincide.

"I have no intention of hurting her," he told Kristy honestly.

"You think Jack intended to hurt me?"

"I think Jack was insane to marry you."

Kristy's eyes flashed.

"You know what I mean. He went into it for all the wrong reasons."

"Unlike you and Sinclair?" She didn't give him a chance to respond. "She's going to fall for you, Hunter. You're wining her and dining her and she's thinking she's become a fairy princess. How could she help but fall for you?"

"Point taken." Hunter tried a turn with Kristy, and she easily followed his lead. But it wasn't the same as dancing with Sinclair. It was nothing at all like dancing with Sinclair.

"So, what are you going to do?"

"For tonight—" Hunter took a deep breath and made up his mind "—I'm going to switch rooms with you and Jack."

Kristy and Jack were on a different floor of the hotel. And Hunter knew deep down in his heart that the adjoining door with Sinclair would prove too much of a temptation.

"You're a good man, Hunter," said Kristy, her eyes softening.

"Can I have that in writing? It might sway your husband."

"I'm talking about your moral code, not your business savvy."

"Nice."

"But that's none of my business."

"The push and pull has been going on a long time," said Hunter. "Jack, Gramps, the investors gripe and complain, but they take the dividends all the same."

"Your investments make dividends?"

"And capital gains, each and every one of them."

Kristy shook her head in obvious confusion. "Then why—"

"Because they think the odds are catching up with me, and they're sure I'm taking the entire flagship down one day."

"Will you?"

"Not planning on it." He danced her toward Jack and Sinclair. He might not be able to hold Sinclair in his bed tonight, but he could at least hold her on the dance floor until the clock struck midnight.

Nine

Nine

When Hunter had squeezed her hand in front of Kristy and Jack, down in the lobby and said, "See you in the morning," Sinclair knew it was all for show. So she brushed her hair, put on fresh perfume, and changed into the purple negligee from La Petite Fleur. She'd even touched up her face with a few of the Luscious Lavender cosmetics.

So, when the knock came from the adjoining hotel room, she was ready. Pulse pounding, skin tingling, anticipation humming along her nervous system, she opened the door.

"Hey, sis," sang Kristy. Then she tossed a command over her shoulder, "Avert your eyes, Jack."

Sinclair's jaw dropped open.

"I brought a nice Chardonnay." Kristy waved an open bottle in the air. "You got some glasses?"

Kristy breezed past her, and Sinclair met Jack's eyes.

"Jack," Kristy warned.

"Sorry," he called, lowering his gaze.

Sinclair turned to her sister. "What on earth—"

"You might want to shut the door," said Kristy.

"Where's Hunter?"

"We traded rooms."

Sinclair swung the door shut, battling her shock. "I can't believe you would—"

"It was his idea. He asked me to do it."

Why would Hunter ask to trade rooms? "Did you threaten him?" Sinclair asked suspiciously.

Kristy poured two glasses of wine. "Yeah. I did, so he backed off. Does that sound like Hunter?"

"No," Sinclair admitted. Hunter refused to back down from Jack and his grandfather. He sure wasn't going to back down from Kristy.

Kristy rounded the small coffee table and flopped down on one of the armchairs. "He traded rooms, because he doesn't want to hurt you. I admire that."

"He's not going to hurt me." Hurting was the furthest thing from what would happen between Hunter and Sinclair tonight.

Kristy took in Sinclair's outfit. "Well, he'd sure be doing something with you dressed like that."

Sinclair glanced down. "What? So we bought a few things at La Petite Fleur."

Dressed in a snazzy workout suit, Kristy curled her legs beneath her.

"And where do you see this thing going?"

"I haven't thought about it," Sinclair lied. She'd pictured everything from an "hasta la vista, baby" to a tear-stained goodbye, to a white dress and a cathedral.

"You work for him."

"I know. Don't you think I know?"

"Reality check," said Kristy. "Hunter's not a one-woman man."

"Reality check," Sinclair countered. "I'm not a one-man woman."

"Not before now."

"Do you honestly think I've fallen in love with him?" She hadn't.

"Not yet," said Kristy. "But you're taking an awfully big risk. You'll have to work with him afterward no matter what. With all the money he's invested in Castlebay, he's going to have to spend one heck of a lot of time at Lush Beauty. He *needs* this to work. And if your past becomes a problem, guess who's going to be gone?"

"You think Hunter would fire me?" Talk about extrapolating facts to the worst-case scenario.

"I think he might have to make a choice."

Sinclair took a long swallow of her wine, hating the fact that the scenario was possible.

She spun the stem of her glass around her fingertips. "What does Jack think?"

"Jack thinks Hunter's playing with fire. He's been reckless and impulsive before."

Sinclair tipped up the glass for another swallow. Reckless and impulsive, everybody seemed to agree on that, including Hunter.

"And it was his idea to switch rooms with you?" Sinclair confirmed.

Kristy nodded.

Sinclair played around with that little fact. Switching rooms meant Hunter thought it wouldn't last. Chivalrous of him to back off, really. Telling, but chivalrous.

"Did you get my message from last night?"

"I did."

Sinclair couldn't keep the hurt from her voice. "Why didn't you call me?" At least then she would have known to give Hunter a heads-up.

"I'd already told Jack what you said."

Sinclair watched her sister closely. "And Jack told you not to call me."

Kristy hesitated, then she gave a nod. It was her turn to drain her glass.

"Men coming between us," said Sinclair. "Who'd have thought?"

"He's my husband. And Hunter's his cousin. And this was family business."

"And I'm not family."

"Not the Osland family."

Sinclair nodded. "Not the Osland family."

Kristy tucked her blond hair behind her ears. "You sure you're not in love with him?"

She wasn't. Of all the things going on here, that, at least, wasn't an issue. "We've known each other a week. We've slept together exactly twice."

"I fell for Jack in a weekend."

"Are you *trying* to talk me into loving Hunter?"

"I'm wondering if you should come back to New York with me tomorrow."

"My makeover's not done yet."

She wouldn't run away. But she could keep it professional. They'd finish the dance lessons, take the planned tours of Castlebay locations, then she'd return to the U.S. and normal life. Her career would get back on track, and Hunter would go out and make more millions.

No big deal. No huge goodbye. They'd settle into their respective lives, and he'd forget all about her.

* * *

The next morning, as arranged, Sinclair entered the hotel dining room for a goodbye breakfast with Kristy. The maître d' recognized her and escorted her through the maze of diners, around the corner to a huge balcony overlooking the atrium.

There, the entire contingent of Oslands sat at a round table, heads bent together, talking rapidly and earnestly, frustration clear on Jack's and Cleveland's faces.

When Jack spotted Sinclair, he touched Cleveland's arm. The man looked up and stopped talking. Hunter and Kristy caught on, and all four shifted back. Forced smiles appeared on their faces.

She'd never felt so much like an outsider in her life.

Kristy stood. "Morning, sis." She came forward for a quick hug, gesturing to a chair between her and Cleveland.

Sinclair pointed to the way she'd come in. "I can…"

"Don't be silly," said Kristy. She shot a glance to the men.

They all came to their feet, talking overtop of one another as they insisted she stay.

She looked at Hunter, but his gaze was guarded. The intimacy was gone, and she couldn't find a clue as to whether she should be here or go.

Hunter moved around Cleveland to pull out her chair.

Sinclair sat down.

"Where were we?" asked Kristy. "Oh, yes. We were talking about the cruise."

Jack smoothly picked up on his wife's cue. "Can you be ready tomorrow afternoon?" he asked. "The captain could wait in port until Tuesday morning, but it's best if we keep the ship on schedule."

Cleveland sat in sullen silence.

"Do you think I should pick up a few sundresses before we go?" Kristy chirped. "Or maybe do a little—"

"This is ridiculous," said Sinclair.

Everyone looked at her.

She started to rise. "I'm going back to my—"

Reaching behind Cleveland, Hunter grabbed her arm. "You're not going anywhere."

She stared at him, then included everybody. "You have things to talk about. And it's not Kristy's sundresses."

Jack spoke up. "I happen to have a passionate interest in Kristy's sundresses. More so in her bikinis."

"Sinclair's right," barked Cleveland.

"Thank you," said Sinclair.

He swiveled in his chair to face her. "But she doesn't have to leave."

Sinclair didn't know what to say to that. The hollow buzz of voices from the atrium washed over her while his piercing eyes held her in place.

"I understand you were involved in the Castlebay acquisition."

"Gramps," warned Hunter.

"Well?" Cleveland pressed. "Were you or were you not?"

Sinclair struggled not to squirm under his probe, excruciatingly aware that this man held controlling interest in Osland International, which held controlling interest in Lush Beauty Products, and he could end her career with the snap of his fingers.

"Yes," she answered. "It was my idea."

"It was *my* idea," said Hunter.

"But—"

"Sinclair may have mentioned something about a single spa in New York. But I approached Castlebay. I did the research. I agreed to the price. And I signed the check. So, back off on Sinclair."

Cleveland turned to Hunter. "I'm interested in how much influence she has over you."

"None," said Hunter. "It was a business decision, and it was a good one. You read the reports."

Sinclair tried not to react to that statement. Of course it was a business decision. And she never assumed she had any influence over Hunter. But, somehow, his words hurt all the same.

Cleveland nodded. "I read the reports. The problem is cash flow."

"I just told you, borrow against the Paraguay mines."

"With currency fluctuations and the political instability? Do you want Osland International to fall down like a house of cards, boy?"

"Jack could give up the cruise ships he's just acquired," said Hunter.

"Jack cleared the cruise ship with the Board of Directors," Jack drawled.

Sinclair was afraid to move. She wanted to speak up, to explain. But couldn't summon the words.

Kristy leaned over and whispered in her ear. "Relax."

"We have options," Hunter spat.

"Are you kidding?" Sinclair hissed to her sister.

"They do this all the time," said Kristy.

"Castlebay is going to turn Lush Beauty into a gold mine," said Hunter with grim determination. "And *that's* what you sent me to do there."

"I sent you there to apologize to Sinclair."

Sinclair couldn't hold back. "He doesn't need—"

"You don't want a piece of this," Hunter warned her. Then

he set his sights back on his grandfather. "Next time you have a problem with my behavior, talk to me."

"Why? You never listen."

"And where the hell do you think I might have inherited that trait?"

"Insolent young pup," Cleveland muttered.

"Wait for it," Kristy whispered.

Cleveland squared his shoulders. "Don't you forget who built this company from an empty warehouse and a corner store."

"And you took exactly the same risks as me back then," Hunter practically shouted. "You didn't check with the Board of Directors, and you didn't convene a thirty-person legal panel with six months' lead time. You flew by the seat of your pants. *That's* how you built this company."

"Times have changed," said Cleveland.

"Maybe," Hunter allowed.

"And our current cash position is appalling."

"I'm not returning the cruise ships," said Jack, his arm going around his wife. "Kristy's buying a sundress."

"You're not returning the cruise ships," Cleveland agreed. "Hunter's going to fix this."

Hunter stared stonily at his coffee mug.

"I think we can join one of the ships in Fiji by the day after tomorrow," said Kristy in a perky voice that was completely at odds with the conversation.

Jack stroked her hair. "You'll look great on the beach," he cheerfully told her, clearly picking up on her lead.

Kristy elbowed Sinclair.

"Uh… What color bikini?" Sinclair tried, unable to take her eyes off Hunter.

"Purple," said Kristy. "And maybe a matching hat."

"Did you put any hats in the spring collection?" asked Cleveland. "I think we should start a new trend."

Hunter drew a deep breath. "Hats were up across the board at Sierra Sanchez last fall. Gramps may have a point."

Jack took a drink of his coffee and signaled for the waiter to bring refills, while Cleveland picked up his menu.

Sinclair glanced from person to person in complete astonishment. That was it? The blowup was over, and they were all having breakfast?

Hunter's family was insane.

Hunter could handle his family.

What he couldn't handle was his growing desire to be with Sinclair. When Gramps left and Jack and Kristy checked out of the Ciel D'Or Hotel yesterday, Hunter gave up the room adjoining Sinclair's, keeping the one on the top floor instead.

It didn't help.

Or maybe it did.

He still wanted to hold her, talk to her and laugh with her all night long. But being ten floors away made it harder for him to act on those impulses.

Before she left, Kristy had given him a lecture. Telling him in no uncertain terms to put Sinclair's interests first. Office affairs never ended well, and it was Sinclair who stood to get hurt. So, if Hunter cared for her at all, even just a little bit, he'd back off and let her get her career under control.

Then, just in case the lecture didn't take, Kristy had pointed out that things generally went bad for men whose cousins-in-law were gunning for them, as well. While Hunter was willing to take his chances with Cleveland and Jack's wrath, he didn't want to cross Kristy.

Plus, he cared for Sinclair. He cared for her more than just a little bit. Although he'd never admit it, she had influenced him in the Castlebay deal. Every time his instincts had twitched, or when Richard had pointed out a potential weakness in the deal, Hunter had seen Sinclair's smiling face, and he'd imagined the rush of telling her they owned the spas.

Castlebay wasn't a bad deal. But it wasn't a "pull out all the stops and get the papers signed in forty-eight hours" deal, either.

Yes, he cared about Sinclair. And he wanted her happy. And sleeping with her wasn't going to make her happy in the long run—even though it would make him ecstatic, short term.

Right now, he heard her heels tap on the hardwood floor. He glanced over to see her cross the dance studio in strappy black sandals and a bright, gauzy blue dress that flowed in points around her tanned calves. The skirt sections separated to give him glimpses of her thighs as she walked.

The dance instructor cued up the music, and Hunter braced himself.

"Ready?" Sinclair asked, her eyes sparkling sapphires that matched the brilliance of the dress.

He took a breath and held out his arms.

"You need to remember," he told her, watching them together in the big mirror. "From the minute you walk into the ball to the minute you leave, you're on stage. Roger will be watching what you do and how you do it."

"You're making me nervous again," she complained. But she glanced into the nearest mirror, then pulled back her shoulders and straightened her spine.

Hunter splayed his palm flat against her back. "Don't be nervous. Look into my eyes. Pay attention to my hand. We're in this together."

She met his gaze, and longing catapulted within him. Other

than a chaste peck on the cheek, he'd kept to himself since Kristy's lecture. But now Sinclair was fully in his arms. The back of her dress dipped to a low V, and his thumb brushed her bare skin.

He felt her shiver at the touch, and her reaction ratcheted up his own desire. Damn. He had to get his mind on the dancing.

Hunter led her through the opening steps.

"Go back, Sinclair," the instructor said. "Now left foot. Shoulders parallel. That's good. Get ready for the turn."

Hunter turned her, and Sinclair didn't stumble. Hunter smiled at her achievement.

"Promenade," said the instructor, and Hunter slipped his arm around Sinclair's waist, settling his hand above her hipbone.

"Good start," said the instructor. "Now, take it away, Hunter. Let's see what we've got to work with."

"Watch out," Hunter smiled at Sinclair, pulling her with his fingers, then pushing with the heel of his hand. She moved to the right, then the left, then backward, then into a turn. And she stumbled.

"Again," said the instructor, and Hunter started over.

She got it right. Then nailed it again.

After four times through the pattern, Hunter altered the ending and caught her by surprise.

"Hey," she protested.

"Stick with me. It's boring if we never do anything new."

"We never do anything at all, anymore," she muttered under her breath.

He didn't think he could have heard her right. "Excuse me?"

"Nothing."

He switched her to a cuddle position. He leaned down, intending to murmur in her ear. She wanted to flirt? He was there.

"Head high," the instructor called.

Hunter corrected his posture and caught her smirk.

He went back to the basic pattern, then changed it up, then whirled her through an underarm turn, her skirts flaring around her knees.

"You are absolutely gorgeous," he whispered.

"Thank you," she said on a sigh. "But I'm tired of being gorgeous."

The song faded to an end.

"What do you mean?" he asked.

She fingercombed her hair. "Restaurants and dances and fancy clothes are all well and good. But I want to kick back. Maybe hop into sweats, watch a sappy movie and cook something for myself." She pouted prettily. "I miss cooking."

"I don't miss cooking."

"That's because you're spoiled."

"I'm not spoiled."

She looked pointedly around the big, mirrored room. "We're having a private dance lesson."

The music started, and he took her into his arms once again, not fighting his feelings so much anymore.

"That," he said as he squared his shoulders and checked their lines, "is because *I'm* spoiling *you.*"

She seemed to contemplate his words as the notes ascended. "That is also true."

Hours later, Sinclair glanced around at the huge arched windows, the kitchenette and the overstuffed leather furniture. "All this time you've had a kitchen?" she asked Hunter.

Hunter set two grocery bags down on the marble counter in the small kitchen alcove while Sinclair checked out the other rooms.

"Jack likes nice things for Kristy," Hunter called.

"Kristy doesn't need a four-person whirlpool," Sinclair called back. "I've been camping with that woman."

"The whirlpool's nice," said Hunter, meeting Sinclair in the main room.

She trailed her fingertips along the leather-accented bar. "So, you basically traded me in on a whirlpool and a veranda?"

She'd missed him.

She'd lain awake at night wishing he was there beside her. It would be nice to make love, sure. But she also wanted to feel his warmth, hear his breathing, even read the morning paper side by side.

"Don't forget the microwave," he said, and picked up one of the hotel phones, punching in a number.

"Well, then. No wonder. I can hardly compete with a microwave." She kicked off her high-heeled sandals and eased up onto a bar stool, arranging the gauzy skirt around her legs. She'd had fun dancing tonight. It seemed as if it was finally coming together. She was reading Hunter's signals, and she found herself looking forward to meeting him on the dance floor at the ball.

Of course, she'd have to dance with other people. But she'd savor the moments with Hunter, even though it would signal the end of their personal relationship. She couldn't see them spending much time together once they were back in New York.

She tried not to feel sad about that. Instead, she gazed at him across the room, taking a mental snapshot of his relaxed posture and smiling face.

He spoke into the telephone receiver. "I'm looking for some ladies' sportswear."

Sinclair turned her attention to the gilded mirror and the assortment of liquors behind the bar. In the meantime, she knew how to make a great mushroom sauce for their chicken breasts, if they had…there it was. Calvados brandy.

She slipped down and padded around the end of the bar. She doubted she could compete with the chefs who must cook for Hunter, but she'd give it her best try.

"Ladies' sweatpants," said Hunter. "Gray."

Sinclair grinned to herself, snagging the bottle of brandy. As he'd done so many times, he was giving her exactly what she'd asked for.

"Maybe a tank top?" He looked at her, and she nodded her agreement.

"Size small," he said while she headed for the kitchenette, scoping out the few cupboards for dishes. They were going to have a relaxing evening. Just the two of them. She hadn't felt this relaxed in weeks.

"Great," he said into the phone. "No, that should do it."

"A baking dish," Sinclair called, finding plates, silverware and glasses.

Hunter relayed the message.

"Oh, and a pot," she said. "With a lid."

"One pot and one lid," Hunter said into the phone. Then he looked to Sinclair. "That everything?"

She nodded, closing the cupboards and removing the groceries from the sacks.

"Thank you," Hunter said into the phone. Then he hit the off button.

"Wine?" he asked Sinclair.

"You bet." She'd worked hard today. In fact, she'd worked hard all week. Glamming up was no easy business.

"Red or white?"

"You pick."

"Mouton Rothschild," he decided, retrieving a bottle from the wine rack and snagging the corkscrew from the bar top.

"What's the occasion?"

"You," he said, slicing off the foil cover. "In gray sweat-pants." Then he twisted the corkscrew.

"If that doesn't cry out for a fine beverage, I don't know what does."

"Me, neither." He popped the cork and poured the dark liquid into two wide-mouthed wineglasses. Then he carried them to the counter where she was working.

"Know how to make a salad?" she asked, setting out lettuce, tomatoes, peppers and cucumber.

"Nope," he answered, sipping the wine.

"Know how to eat a salad?"

"Of course."

She opened a drawer, pulled out a chopping knife and set it on the counter. "Then wing it."

"Hey, you were the one bent on giving up luxury."

"And you get to help."

"I bought the sweatpants," he grumbled.

"Don't forget to wash everything."

Hunter stared blankly at the assortment of vegetables. "Maybe I should call the chef."

"And how would that be a home-cooked meal?"

"He'd be in our home while he cooked it."

Sinclair pulled in her chin, peering at him through the tops of her eyes. "Shut up and start chopping."

"Okay," he agreed with a tortured sigh. "It's your funeral."

She removed the butcher's paper from the chicken breasts. "You can't kill me with a salad."

"I have never, I mean never, cooked anything in my life."

She stared at him in disbelief. "Don't you ever get hungry, like late at night?"

"Sure."

"And?"

"And I call the kitchen." He looked doubtful as he un-wrapped a yellow pepper.

"You seriously need a reality check."

"I seriously need a chef."

"Peel off the label, then wash the pepper, cut it vertically and take out the seeds."

Hunter blinked at her.

She rattled into one of the bags, looking for spices. "That's not going to work."

"What's not going to work?"

"That, oh-so-pathetic, lost-little-boy expression."

He gave up and peeled off the label, then turned to the sink. "It's tried and true on about a dozen nannies."

"You must have been incorrigible."

"I was delightful."

"I'm sure."

She spiced the chicken breasts, then chopped up the mush-rooms, while Hunter butchered a number of innocent veg-etables beyond recognition.

"Did you get cream?" she asked, peering into the bottom of the sack.

"Over here." He reached around her, and her face came up against his chest. His clean scent overwhelmed her, while her breasts brushed his stomach. Everything inside her contracted with desire.

"Here you go." He set the carton of cream on the counter in front of her. If he'd noticed the breast brush, he didn't let on. She, on the other hand, was still tingling from the contact.

She turned away and set the oven temperature. It was too early to make the sauce, so she put the cream in the half-sized fridge and moved to put some distance between her and Hunter.

"Can we get a movie?" she asked.

"There's a DVD library behind the couch. Or pay-per-view if you want something current."

"A classic?" she asked, skirting the couch.

"It's your night," he responded. "If it was mine, the fantasy would include waiters."

It was on the tip of her tongue to ask for details about his fantasy night, but she quickly realized that would take them down a dangerous road.

A knock sounded.

"The sweatpants," said Hunter from where he was running the cucumber under cold water.

Sinclair left the DVD library to go for the door.

She took the sweatpants and tank top into Hunter's bedroom, stripping off her dancing dress and hanging it in the closet. The V back of the dress hadn't allowed for a bra, so she wasn't wearing one. The sweats were loose and rode low on her hips. While the pale-purple-and-gray-striped tank top left a strip of bare skin on her abdomen. But the cotton fabric was soft and cool, and she felt more relaxed than she had in days.

"You should take off your tie," she said to Hunter as she reemerged into the living room.

He glanced up, and his gaze stopped on her outfit for a few seconds.

"Good idea." He dried his hands then worked open the knot. He unbuttoned his cuffs and rolled up the sleeves.

She crouched in front of the DVD rack. *"Notting Hill?"* she asked. "Or *While You Were Sleeping? Sweet Home Alabama?"*

"Is that the chick-flick shelf?"

"How about *Die Hard?"*

"Now *that's* a movie."

"Fine, but nobody ever got lucky watching *Die Hard.*"

"Am I getting lucky?"

She ignored him. "Here we go. *The Last of the Mohicans.*"

He nodded. "Good compromise."

She pulled it from the shelf. "Action, adventure, emotion and romance."

"Sounds like a winner to me."

"It's not very funny."

"Apparently, we can't have everything." He stepped back from the counter. "However, we have achieved salad."

She walked over to check it out. The lettuce pieces were too large, the peppers were practically pureed, and there was a puddle of water forming at the bottom of the bowl.

"Good job."

"Thank you. But I'm pretty sure it's going to be a once-in-a-lifetime experience."

She snagged a crooked slice of cucumber and popped it in her mouth. "Then I'll be sure to savor it."

He looked down into her eyes. "Excellent idea," he said, and her breath caught at the tone of his voice. "Savoring those experiences that are rare."

Ten

Dinner over, Hunter and Sinclair each found a comfortable spot on the leather couch. They had a box of chocolate truffles between them, and another bottle of Château Rothschild on the coffee table. He would have liked to draw her into his arms, or into his lap, or at least over beside him. But until she sent a signal, he didn't intend to make a move.

She curled up, her legs beneath her, and her pert breasts rounded out against the tight tank top. He could make out the outline of her nipples in the dim light, and he stared at them with a fatalistic longing. Her shoulders were tanned and smooth, her bare waist and cute belly button were nipped in above the low cut pants. And he could see the barest hint of her satin panties along the line of her hip.

She reached for a chocolate. "Did you try the Grande Marnier?" Her lips wrapped halfway around the dark globe, and she bit down with an appreciate groan.

He wasn't going to make it through the movie.

There was absolutely no way he was going to make it through the movie.

"Here." She held out the other half of the chocolate.

He leaned forward, and she popped it into his mouth. Then she licked the remaining chocolate cream from her fingertips.

"Good?" she asked.

He nodded, unable to form an actual word.

The American frontier bloomed up on the wide screen.

Sinclair reached for her wine. "Here we go."

He didn't even glance at the colorful screen. Instead, he stared at her profile, remembering what it felt like to kiss her lips, to taste the smooth skin of her shoulders and breasts, to stroke his fingers along the most intimate parts of her body.

She sipped her wine, and he watched her swallow. She smiled, then frowned, her eyes squinting down in reaction to the story.

"You done?" he asked, moving the chocolate box to the coffee table, clearing his path. If he had an opportunity to move closer, he'd take it in a split second.

She glanced at the box. Then she nodded.

Using the excuse of replacing the lid, he eased toward the middle of the couch, then he settled back to bide his time while the story unfolded.

As the heroine's party made their way through the bush and the music signaled the tension and danger, Sinclair pushed herself to the back of the couch.

Hunter moved a little closer, stretching his arm across the back. "You okay?" he asked.

She nodded, gaze not leaving the screen.

The first attack came, and she jerked in reaction. Hunter

covered her shoulder in comfort, and her hand came up to squeeze his. Her skin was soft and warm against his palm, and her fingers were delicate where they entwined with his own.

The story moved on until the hero and heroine were pinned down in the woods. They joined forces, and Sinclair sighed. Hunter had to admit this was a much better date movie than *Die Hard*.

He shifted closer still, so that their thighs brushed together. When, under gunfire, the hero and heroine finally came together to make love, Sinclair leaned her head on Hunter's shoulder.

Unable to resist, he kissed the top of her head, and wrapped an arm tight around her.

By the time the action got bloody, she was burying her face in his chest. And, at the resolution, she relaxed, molding against his body while she tipped her chin up to look him in the eyes.

"Hey," he said gruffly.

"Inspiring story," she returned.

Neither moved away, and they stared at each other in silence, her eyes reflecting the longing in his blood.

"Your sister's right," he finally offered in a last ditch attempt to be a gentleman.

Sinclair didn't answer, instead her hand crept up along his chest, finding the bare skin of his neck, and caressing it in a way that made him groan.

"My sister's sleeping with your cousin," she said.

Hunter didn't understand the point, but he couldn't formulate the right question.

Sinclair stretched up to kiss the corner of his mouth. "That means she can afford to be right." She gave him a swift kiss on the center of his lips.

He automatically puckered in response.

"I, on the other hand, am in the mood to be very, very wrong."

"So am I," he breathed, scooping his hand beneath her bottom and easing her into a reclining position beside him.

His lips came down on hers with all the purpose in the world.

Then he stripped off her tank top, wrapping his arms around her bare back and pulling her breasts flush against his body.

"I want you so bad," he rasped, kissing her collarbone, her breasts, the tight pebble of her nipple that he'd been watching for two long, painful hours.

"I've missed you," she confessed. "I don't care that we have to go back. I don't care that it has to end."

He slipped a hand beneath her sweatpants, beneath her satin panties, to her bare buttocks. "Nothing's going to end tonight. Not for a very, very long time."

She smiled up at him, her blue eyes turning to midnight sky as her fingers tugged his shirt from his waistband. "I want to touch every inch of your body."

"Good."

"I want you inside me for hours."

"Better."

"I want to make love so long and so hard…."

Hunter kissed her mouth, over and over, completely speechless with desire.

"What should I do?" she breathed.

"You're already doing it."

His hot gaze took in her bare breasts. He stripped off the sweat pants and stared at the satin panties he'd glimpsed earlier. He ran his hand down her thigh, along her calf, over the arch of her foot.

She managed to slip off his shirt.

Her hands went to his chest, stroking upward, pausing on his nipples. "I don't think we'll be waxing," she said, and he chuckled at her joke.

He ran his hand up her calf again. "Somebody's been waxing."

"It doesn't hurt that much."

"Glad you're tough." He ran the hand back down. "Really glad you're tough."

"Smooth, huh?"

"Smooth as silk." He trickled his fingers up her thigh, slipping them beneath her panties, teasing the smooth skin near the top.

Sinclair gasped at the sensation, arching her back, plastering her body against his, feeling the rough texture of his slacks against her thighs.

"You are amazing," he gasped.

"You are… You are…" She didn't even have words for it.

"Impatient," he supplied, pushing his way out of his slacks.

"Thank goodness." She smiled.

But he stopped, their naked bodies flush against each other. He rubbed a thumb across her sensitive lips, kissed them thoroughly, then rubbed it once more. "You sure you're ready?"

She nodded. Her entire body tingled in anticipation. Hunter. She was getting Hunter again. Finally.

He stroked her thighs, parting them, then slowly pushed his way inside.

A powerful, unfamiliar feeling surged through her body. She tunneled her fingers into his hair, she clutched his back, arching against him, delving into their kiss until the rest of the world disappeared.

"Damn," he muttered, pulling back ever so slightly, blinking his eyes. He glanced down to where their bodies met. "This has to last."

"Make it last," she whispered. Forever and ever and ever.

She kissed his forehead, his eyelids, his cheeks. Then she got serious again on his mouth.

His fingers moved to the small of her back. Then his hands cupped her bottom and he rocked her pelvis as his hard length moved in and out. The low buzz in her body ratcheted up to a roar. Shots of sparkling heat radiated out from her center. Her breath came in small gasps against his lips.

Her hands fisted on his back. Her thighs tightened, her eyes fluttered closed, and she rocked herself hard into his rhythm.

"I...can't..." she panted. "Oh...please..."

He lifted her ever so slightly, changing the angle, making her eyes pop open in wonder.

They both stilled, faces mere inches apart, staring at each other, gasping the same air. And then he moved, and she groaned, and her universe contracted to the place where their bodies were joined.

She wrapped her arms around his neck and held on tight, inhaling his scent as deep as she could manage, tasting the salt of his skin, feeling his taught muscles surround her and block out the world.

They both made it last, refusing to give in to the ultimate pleasure as the minutes ticked by and slick sweat gathered between their bodies.

Hunter's name began pounding in her brain. An exquisite pulse started low, becoming more insistent, forcing a moan from her lips and making her hips buck uncontrollably.

He whispered her name, and she was lost.

He followed her, her name on his lips over and over and over again.

* * *

They switched to the bed and made love again. Sinclair clung to him with all her might, wishing she could hold off the morning.

But when they finally separated, gasping and exhausted, the sun was an orange glow on the horizon.

"Now *that* was reckless and impulsive," said Hunter.

"Your family should really stop trying to beat those impulses out of you."

"You want to tell them that?"

"I do. Hand me your cell phone."

He did.

She pressed Jack's speed-dial button before Hunter whisked it out of her hand.

"I thought you were bluffing," he said.

She grinned. "And I thought you could wrestle a six-foot alligator."

"Okay," he groaned, dropping the phone on the bedside table. "All kidding aside. We've got trouble."

"We certainly do."

He propped himself up on his elbow and traced a line from her shoulder to her wrist. "Question is," he drawled softly, "what do we do about it?"

"You're still my boss," she said.

"I am."

"We still can't have an office fling."

"Agreed."

"Of course, we're not in the office now."

"I like the way you're thinking."

She popped up on her elbow, facing him, matching his posture. "We could keep it up until we get home."

Hunter watched her for a few minutes, concern flitting across his expression. "Kristy's afraid you'll fall for me."

"I know she is."

He took a breath as if he was steeling himself. "You gonna fall for me, Sinclair?"

"Don't flatter yourself," she quickly put in. "You're too reckless and impulsive to be a long-term bet."

"Plus, I lie."

"Plus," she agreed with a nod, "you lie."

He reached out to stroke her cheek with the pad of his thumb, brushing back her hair.

"I don't want to hurt you," he said.

She squelched her softer feelings. It was a fling or nothing, and that was the hard, cold truth of the matter. And she didn't want nothing, so she was taking the fling.

"What if I hurt you?" she suggested in return, just to keep things fair.

"I don't think Kristy cares so much about that." He paused. "We've got three whole days until the Valentine's ball."

"And two whole nights to go with them."

He kissed her nose. "So we're decided then?"

She nodded against him. "I think our only hope is to get it out of our system."

"Agreed."

Sinclair pushed to a sitting position. "We're going to see the spas today, right?"

"Paris, London and Brussels."

"Then we should get going."

Hunter groaned, tugging her back into place and pulling the covers over them. "First, we sleep."

"The sooner we get going, the sooner we get back."

He paused and opened one eye. "To this big, lovely bed."

"In this big, lovely suite."

"Can we get room service this time?"

"Poor baby," she cooed, drawing his fingertips to her lips and kissing them one by one. "Did you cut yourself chopping?"

"It's a time-saving ploy," he explained. "I have my sights set on the whirlpool."

Sinclair hopped up. "I'm in."

They laughed their way through the shower and into their clothes. Hunter had Simon pour on the power across the Channel and then back through Belgium. Sinclair gave the spa managers an orientation to the Luscious Lavender products, put them in touch with Ethan, and with Mary-Anne from distribution, then they hightailed it back to the heart of Paris.

By early evening, they were in the whirlpool.

Hunter pulled Sinclair back into the cradle of his thighs, handing her a flute of champagne and kissing her damp neck. She sighed in contentment, sipping the sweet, bubbly liquid while he lazily scrubbed a foamy loofah sponge over her back.

With his other hand, he touched the jeweled fish on her bracelet.

Sinclair had forgotten she still had it on. She jangled it in front of her eyes. "I think it's my favorite."

He drew her wrist forward to kiss the tender, inside skin. "*This* is my favorite."

"Really?" She pointed to her elbow. "I thought this was your favorite."

He kissed her there. "That, too."

"And this?" she pointed to her shoulder.

"Of course."

"This?" Her neck.

"All of it."

She laughed.

He sat back and his sponge strokes grew longer along her spine.

"Did you get a hold of Roger?" he asked.

"I did. He wasn't thrilled about me delaying my return even longer."

"You mean Chantal's not the wunderkind we all imagined?"

"He didn't complain about her. He said I was setting a bad example."

"By taking your holidays?"

"I guess."

"Want me to talk to him?"

"Oh, yeah. Great idea. Why don't you call him up?"

Sinclair's cell phone chimed.

"If that's Roger," said Hunter. "Tell him I say 'hey.'"

She elbowed Hunter in the ribs, drying one hand before reaching for her phone. "Hello?"

"Hey, you."

Sinclair guiltily pushed Hunter's sponge hand away. "Hi, Kristy."

He continued to rub her back.

"What's up?" asked Kristy.

"Not much. Where are you?"

"Off the coast of New Zealand. We just got cell service back."

"Great."

"So, what are you doing?"

Hunter's hand slipped around to her stomach. "Went to the spa in Brussels today, and the one in London. Met with the managers. Got them all set up for Friday's launch."

"Good for you." Kristy paused. "Hunter still in Paris?"

"He's here. But he was a little standoffish after you left."

Hunter choked back a laugh.

"I guess he came to his senses," said Kristy.

"I guess he did," Sinclair agreed, as the sponge meandered toward her breast. She clutched it to her stomach to stop his progress.

"So, when are you coming home?"

"By the fourteenth, for sure. I need to be there for the ball."

Hunter wrenched his hand free.

Sinclair bit down on her lip to keep from gasping as the sponge brushed between her legs. "I better go," she blurted, grappling for Hunter's meandering hands.

"Anything wrong?"

"Uh, something's boiling on the stove."

"The *stove?*"

"I moved to a suite. Talk to you in a few days." She disconnected.

She turned on him. "Are you crazy?"

"No." He kissed her mouth.

"Do you know what would happen—"

He kissed her again.

"If they—"

He kissed her a third time.

She gave in and wrapped her arms around his neck, turning to press her body into his, the water slick and hot between them.

Hunter's phone rang.

"For the love of—"

"Give me the sponge," she said, holding out her hand.

"Forget it."

She snapped her fingers, then wiggled them in a *give it* motion. "Fair's fair."

He dried his hand, then lifted his phone, at the same time tossing the sponge to her.

She eased back on her heels and snagged it with both hands.

"Hunter Osland," he greeted.

There was a pause. "Hey, Jack." And he grinned at Sinclair, spreading his arms, giving her a wide-open target.

She couldn't decide whether to go for it or not.

Then Hunter's attention clearly shifted to the phone call. "I'd still use the mine as collateral."

He paused.

"Maybe in the short term, sure." He slicked his wet hair back from his forehead.

"Of course he'll be ticked off. Everything ticks him off."

Hunter absently smoothed the droplets of water down Sinclair's arm. She gave up goofing around and curled against him, leaning her head on his shoulder.

"Get in and out before the Paraguay election, and you won't have a problem." Hunter's hand worked its way across her stomach.

She glanced up to see if he was teasing her again, but he seemed absorbed in the call. He wasn't messing with her, just unconsciously caressing her body. She sighed and relaxed against him.

Hunter chuckled, jiggling his chest. "We'll check it out sometime." A pause. "I mean me, of course. *I'll* check it out sometime. None of your business." Hunter's hand squeezed Sinclair. "I'm going now," he said to Jack. "A nap, that's what. Time zone change. Okay by me. I'm turning off my phone. Uh-huh. Goodbye."

He hit the off button with his thumb and held it down until it chimed. Then he dropped it on the shelf beside them and hauled Sinclair up for a kiss.

"You are *so* distracting," he muttered.

"I was being good."

"You were being damn good."

She giggled as his mouth came down, hot and moist and demanding against her own.

The water splashed around the whirlpool in waves as they rediscovered each other's bodies.

Eleven

They were back in the U.S. by midmorning on the fourteenth, and Sinclair couldn't resist checking in at Lush Beauty in one of her new outfits.

Her hair and makeup perfect, she strolled into the office in a slim peacock-blue coat dress, with three-quarter sleeves, leather details on the collar, appliqué pockets, large contrasting silver buttons and high-heeled leather ankle boots. She carried a tiny purse, holding nothing but her cell phone, keys and a credit card.

Amber's jaw literally dropped open as Sinclair crossed through the outer office.

"I was going to check messages," Sinclair called over her shoulder. "You coming to the ball tonight?"

She pushed open her office door and stopped dead.

Chantal sat at her desk, computer open to e-mail, file folders scattered in front of her, and Sinclair's phone to her ear.

Neither woman spoke for a moment.

"Can I call you back?" Chantal said into the phone.

"You're at my desk," said Sinclair.

"You're back early," said Chantal.

Amber apparently recovered her wits and rushed into the office. "Roger asked—"

"I'll be needing it now," Sinclair informed Chantal. "Right now."

Chantal hit a few keys on the computer. "If you'll just give me a few minutes."

"I don't think so," Sinclair stated, walking around the desk. "Those the Valentine's ball files?"

"The Castlebay files," Chantal admitted.

"Oh, good. Just what I wanted." Sinclair dropped her small purse on the desk. She was vindictive enough to put it label up so that Chantal could see it was a Vermachinni.

She inched in closer, crowding the woman until Chantal finally stood up and clicked the close button on her e-mail program. Chantal started to pick up the files.

"You can leave them here," Sinclair told her. "I'll call you if I need anything."

Chantal glared at her.

"Did Roger mention the private party at the Castlebay Spa Manhattan tonight?"

Chantal didn't answer.

Sinclair pursed her lips, knowing full well Roger himself didn't even know about the after party yet.

The woman's eyes glittered black. "Amber said she e-mailed you the catering contracts yesterday?"

"She did. And we've substituted duck for the pheasant. We got rid of the peanut oil because of possible allergies. And the gift bags are now recycled paper, which will stave off any media grab by Earthlife."

Chantal scooped up her briefcase and stomped out of the office.

"Uh," Amber stammered in the wake of Chantal's departure. "Is there anything...you, uh, need?"

Sinclair turned. "Hi," she said to her assistant.

"Coffee?" asked Amber, quickly straightening a pile of magazines on the credenza. "Tea?"

"It's *me*," Sinclair pointed out.

Amber nodded. "Mineral water, maybe?"

"Amber."

"You look..."

Sinclair waved a dismissive hand. "I know. Did you see the ads for the Chastlebay locations? They're having special midnight openings tonight to coincide with the ball over here."

"Sinclair?" came Ethan's voice.

Amber quickly ducked out of the office.

"Good for you," Ethan said to Sinclair.

She assumed he was talking about her appearance and smiled.

"Somebody needs to stand up to Roger."

She realized Ethan was referring to her absence. "All I did was take a vacation."

"On the eve of the product launch."

"True."

"It took a lot of guts."

"I wasn't trying to make a statement." She was merely trying to keep her career path alive.

"I thought you were trying to prove we couldn't live without you."

Sinclair paused. "Can you?"

"It's tough. Not that Roger would ever admit it. Amber really stepped up to the plate."

"Good for her. What about Chantal?"

Ethan cocked his head. "I think she has a future as eye candy."

"That's it?"

"That's it."

Sinclair nodded, glad of Ethan's assessment.

"I really just wanted to give you a high five on the spa deal," said Ethan.

Sinclair grinned and held up her hand.

Ethan smacked his palm against hers. "Hunter's a smart man," he said.

Sinclair nodded her agreement.

"He told me the idea originated with you. So, you know, you probably have a supporter in that corner."

"That's good to know," said Sinclair, trying to keep the secretive glow out of her eyes. Earlier this morning, as the jet taxied to the terminal building at JFK, Hunter had kissed her goodbye and pledged admiration for her business savvy and his support for tonight.

Ethan made for the door. "See you tonight?"

"You will."

As Ethan left, Amber peeked through the doorway. "I hope you don't mind." She took in Sinclair's outfit one more time. "I gave your name and cell phone as an after-hours contact for the caterer tonight."

"Of course I don't mind." That was standard operating procedure.

"Oh, good." Amber disappeared.

Sinclair straightened the Castlebay files, hoping her makeover went a whole lot better tonight than it went today.

Ethan hadn't noticed, Amber was afraid of her, and who knows what Roger had thought? She'd hardly wowed them here on the home front.

* * *

Freshly shaved, in his dress shirt and tuxedo slacks, Hunter looped a silk bow tie around his neck. Sinclair would be wearing her most elegant dress tonight, and he wanted them to go well together. Although they were trying to keep their relationship under wraps—okay, their former relationship under wraps—he seriously wanted her to shine. And he was planning on at least a couple of dances.

He stepped in front of the hallway mirror in the Oslands' New York apartment and leveled the two ends of the tie.

Then his cell phone rang.

He retrieved it from the entry-room table and flipped it open. "This is Hunter."

"Two things," said Jack.

"Go," Hunter replied, squinting at a strand of lint on the crisp white shirt. He brushed it off.

"The incumbent president of Paraguay just dropped dead from a heart attack."

"No kidding?"

"No kidding."

Hunter sat down on the entryway bench. "Did you use the mine as collateral?"

"I did."

"Damn." That was a setback.

"And two," Jack continued. "Frontier Cruise Lines is filing for Chapter Eleven tomorrow morning. There are three ships up for sale in the next twelve hours."

"And our cash position sucks."

"It sucks."

Hunter paused. "You really want to get into the cruise-ship business?"

"Kristy loved it."

Hunter could relate. Sinclair loved the spa business.

Wait.

He shook the comparison out of his mind. He had to get used to thinking of himself and Sinclair as separate entities, not as the same thing.

"Where are you?" he asked Jack.

"Sydney."

Hunter glanced at his watch. "Banks open in London in four hours. You serious about this?"

"What does your gut say?" asked Jack. "You're the quick thinker."

"There's no denying the quality of Frontier ships. And it's an expanding market. We could dovetail Castlebay marketing with a new cruise-line marketing strategy, maybe even put Castlebays on each of the ships." Hunter clicked through a dozen other details in his mind. "You have a sense of the Frontier prices versus market?"

"Fire sale."

"We might be able to do something with the Lithuania electronics plant. Restructure the debt...."

"Gramps will kill us."

"Welcome to my world."

There was silence on the line.

"You know," said Jack. "I think I'm understanding the appeal of this. It's like Vegas."

"Higher stakes," Hunter quipped.

"No kidding," said Jack.

Hunter glanced at his watch. "I'd have to go to London." The Lithuania banking was done through Barclays, and they needed the time-zone jump start to pull it together.

"That a problem?" asked Jack.

Hunter's mind flashed to Sinclair. She'd be all right at

the ball. Truth was, he was merely window dressing tonight. She was *so* ready for this. And, anyway, he could make it up to her later.

"I need to make a couple calls," he said.

"You get the financing in place, and I'll nail down the contracts with Richard."

"Where is he?" asked Hunter.

"L.A."

"Too bad."

"Should I send him to New York?"

"It'd be better if you could get him to London." Hunter paused. "No. Wait. New York will work. Tell him I'll call him around 4:00 a.m."

"Perfect." It was Jack's turn to pause. "And, Hunter?"

"Yeah?"

"Thanks."

"All part of the game, cousin." Hunter disconnected.

He dragged off the bow tie and released the buttons to his shirt.

On the way to the bedroom, he dialed Simon and asked him to have the jet ready. Then he changed into a business suit, put another one into a garment bag and called down to his driver to let him know they'd be heading for the airport.

Sinclair stood in the lobby of the Roosevelt Hotel. She hadn't expected Hunter to pick her up and escort her every movement. It wasn't as if they were on a date. Still, she would have felt a little less self-conscious with somebody at her side.

Tuxedoed men accompanied glittering women dressed in traditional black or brilliant-red evening gowns. The couples were smiling and laughing as they made their way past the sweeping staircase and a central glass sculpture. Plush armchairs dotted the multi-story rotunda, while marble pillars supported sconce lights and settees along a lattice-decorated walkway to the main ballroom.

Flashbulbs popped and cameras rolled as the media vied for footage of the A-list event. The PR person in Sinclair was thrilled with the hoopla, the woman in her was disappointed to be there alone. She squelched the silly, emotional reaction and answered a few questions from a reporter for a popular magazine. But then the reporter spotted someone more exciting and quickly wrapped it up.

"Sinclair," came Sammy Simon's voice.

She turned to see one of the Lush Beauty Lavender suppliers decked out in a black tux and tie.

He took both of her hands in his. "Lovely," he drawled appreciatively, taking in her strapless white satin dress. It had a sweetheart neckline and tiny red hearts scattered over the bodice. The hearts gathered into a vertical, then cascaded down one side of the full skirt.

Sammy kissed her on the cheek. "I had no idea you were a fan of haute couture."

She gave him a laugh. "A little something I picked up in Paris."

He squeezed her hands. "Find me later for a dance." And he joined the throng headed for the party.

"Sinclair," came another voice, and an arm went around her shoulders.

"Mr. Davidson." She greeted the owner of a chain of specialty shops that had featured Lush Beauty Products for years.

"This is my wife, Cynthia."

Sinclair smiled and leaned forward to shake the woman's hand. As she did, Wes Davidson's hand dropped to an uncomfortable level near her hip.

"And one of my store managers, Reginald Pie."

"Nice to meet you, Mr. Pie." Sinclair shook the man's hand.

Wes Davidson spoke up. "It's such a pleasure to see you, Sinclair. I've been meaning to arrange a meeting to talk about the new product lines."

"Absolutely," she agreed.

"I'll call you," he said. "Great to see you looking… so…great."

Mrs. Davidson reddened.

Sinclair gently pulled away. "Oh, look. There's Ethan. I need to say hello. So good to see you Mr. Davidson. Mrs. Davidson."

Sinclair slipped away.

She made a beeline for Ethan. He was talking to two of their distributors.

"But if the price breaks don't work for the small retailers," one of the men was saying, "you're going to compromise your core business."

"Hello, Ethan," Sinclair broke in, grateful to find a safe conversation.

The men stopped talking and turned to stare at her.

"You remember Sinclair," said Ethan.

What a strange thing to say. Of course they remembered her.

"Sinclair," said Ron. "You look incredible."

"Fabulous to see you again," said David.

Then the conversation stopped dead.

Sinclair glanced from one man to the other. "You were talking about price breaks?" she prompted.

David chuckled. "Oh, not tonight," he said. "You look incredible," he repeated Ron's sentiment.

"Thank you." But that didn't mean her brain had stopped working.

There was another strained silence.

"I'll see you all inside?" Sinclair offered.

The men seemed to relax.

"Yes," said David.

"Looking forward to it," said Ron.

Ethan winked.

Sinclair walked away and immediately spotted Chantal.

She was surrounded by admirers, and she didn't seem to mind they were focused on her looks and not on her business savvy. She was a glittering jewel in low-cut bright red, and she seemed to revel in the role.

Sinclair, on the other hand, was having serious reservations about her makeover. Men used to take her seriously. She couldn't remember the last time she felt so awkward in a business conversation.

Her cell phone rang in her evening purse, and she welcomed the distraction. She picked up the call.

"Can you hang on?" she asked, not expecting to be able to hear the answer.

She sought out an alcove behind the concierge desk, next to a bank of phone booths.

"Hello?"

"It's Hunter," came a welcome and familiar voice.

"Hey, you," she responded, her voice softening, and the tension inside her dissipating to nothing. "Are you out front?" She glanced at the foyer, straining to see him coming through the main doors.

"I've had a complication."

"Oh?"

He was going to be late. Sinclair tried to take the news in stride. She really had no expectations of him. At least, she had no right to have any expectations of him. But in that split second, she realized she'd been counting the minutes until he'd arrive.

"I'm on my way to London."

"Now?" she couldn't help but ask.

"There's a couple of cruise ships, and a bankruptcy, and a complication in the Paraguay election."

"I understand," she quickly put in.

"I'm sorry—"

"No need. It's business." She'd been warned he'd hurt her. Hadn't she been warned?

She heard him draw a breath. Traffic sounds came through his end of the phone.

"We only have twelve hours," he told her.

She forced a laugh. "Another quick deal?"

"Jack's on board this time."

"That's good."

"We can get a really great price."

"Of course." She tried to ignore the crushing disappointment pressing down on her chest. She had no right to feel this way. He'd done so much for her already.

"You're great," he told her. "You'll do fine on your own."

"I know," she nodded, realizing how very much she'd been counting on their last dance tonight. There was something about their relationship that cried out for closure—a closure she hadn't yet experienced.

"I wouldn't do it, except—"

"Hunter, stop."

"What?"

"I knew this going in," she pointed out, proud of her even tone.

"Knew what?"

"You. You're reckless and impulsive. You have to fly to London. You have to buy ships. And you have to do it in less than twelve hours. That's you. That what I lo…like about you. Have a great time."

He was silent on the other end.

"You sure?" he finally asked.

"Do I sound sure?"

"Well, yeah."

Her lying skills had obviously improved. "There you go. I'll see you at the office. I gotta go now."

"But—"

"See you." Sinclair clicked off the phone.

She rounded the corner, taking in what now looked like a daunting mix of finely dressed people. And at the same time, she was beginning to fear her colleagues wouldn't take her seriously. While Chantal seemed to be managing the glam persona with aplomb. And now Hunter wasn't even going to show up.

Damn.

She had to stop caring about that.

Had she expected to be Cinderella tonight?

Had she expected he'd sweep the new her onto the dance floor, realize he'd fallen madly in love, and carry her off to happily ever after?

It was a ridiculous fantasy, and Sinclair was horrified to realize it was hers.

Her fingers went to the ruby-and-diamond goldfish bracelet—the one she hadn't taken off in a week.

She'd thought about him every moment while she'd primped tonight. She'd worn a white, whale-boned bustier. It gave body to the dress, but it was also shamelessly sexy. She told herself no one would see it. But, secretly, deep down inside her soul, she'd hoped he would. She'd hoped they'd find an excuse to make love one more time, or maybe a hundred more times.

Truth was, Kristy's fear had proven true. Sinclair had fallen hopelessly in love with Hunter. Hunter, on the other hand, skipped the ball to make a new business deal.

Her eyes burned while a knot of shame formed in her belly. Suddenly the designer clothes felt like zero protection for her broken heart.

She should have stuck with her regular wardrobe. Beneath her skirts and blazers and sensible blouses, she was in control of her world. People saw what she wanted them to see, and they respected what she represented. She was a fool to think she could beat Chantal at her own game. And she was a fool to think she could hold on to Hunter.

Reckless and impulsive. She'd heard those words so many times. There was nothing Sinclair could offer him that would compare to a high-risk, hundred-million-dollar deal in London at midnight.

She stepped away from the alcove, determined to get this horrible evening over with as soon as possible.

Twelve

The jets taking off from JFK squealed above Hunter's head as his driver circled his way through the terminals. He had his PDA set to calculator, running the numbers he knew he needed banking software to properly compute.

But the mini screen kept blurring in front of his eyes. He was seeing Sinclair in her white and red dress. The piping along the neckline. The teardrop diamonds. The ruby necklace. Her expression when she'd realized the massive ruby was real.

He chuckled at that, particularly the part where he realized she still liked the goldfish bracelet better.

He wondered if she'd worn it tonight.

He wondered if she'd got her makeup just right.

Had her hair behaved?

Were her feet getting tired?

She'd gamely practiced for hours in those high shoes, but he knew she didn't like them.

He wondered who she was dancing with right now, and quickly acknowledged that he cared. Something pulled tight inside him at the image of someone else holding her, their broad hand splayed across her back, another man's jacket nearly brushing her breasts, the jerk's lips whispering secrets into her ear.

If he was in the room, he'd probably rip her from the guy's arms.

His cell phone beeped.

"Hunter Osland," he greeted.

"Hey, Hunter."

"Sinclair?" His heart lifted.

"It's Kristy."

"Oh."

"Were you expecting Sinclair?"

"No."

"Because I think she's at that ball tonight."

"She is." He shifted in the backseat of the car. All alone at the ball.

"I just talked to Jack," said Kristy.

Sinclair was all alone, because Hunter had let her down.

"Jack's cell was running low on battery power," Kristy continued.

It wasn't like he'd had a choice. Osland International needed him, and his grandfather was always after him to be more dependable. That's what he was doing by helping Jack.

"Jack wants you to call Richard for him."

This was being dependable—and patient and methodical. Those were the other things his grandfather wanted.

Kristy's words rambled together on the other end of the

phone without making a whole lot of sense. "He said you'd know why."

Though he'd also been patient and methodical when he convinced Sinclair to get a makeover, then when he took her to Europe, then when he bought her clothes, then when he taught her to dance. He also made sure she was completely ready to face Roger and the rest of Lush Beauty.

"Hunter?" prompted Kristy.

And…then he'd abandoned her for the first exciting project that came along.

Oh no.

He pictured her in his mind, stunningly gorgeous and all alone, other men circling like wolves.

Was he out of his mind?

"No!"

"*What?*" came Kristy's worried voice.

The Sinclair project wasn't over. There were things left to do for her. A whole lot of things left to for her, patient and methodical things left to do for her, some of them involving the rest of their natural lives.

"Hunter? What's going on."

"Tell Jack I'm sorry."

"Huh?"

"Tell him I can't call Richard. I can't go to London. If he can't work it out himself, well, tell him there'll be other cruise ships."

"Other cruise ships?" Kristy parroted in confusion.

"For once in my life I'm not going to be reckless and impulsive. I'm going to be dependable." Why hadn't he thought about that before? He was such a fool.

"What are you talking about?" Kristy was obviously trying to be patient.

"I have to go see Sinclair."

"How'd Sinclair get into this?"

"Because," Hunter hesitated. Part of him didn't want to say it out loud, and part of him wanted to shout it from the rooftops. "I'm in love with your sister," he admitted to Kristy. "I'll have to call you back."

Then he disconnected and caught the driver's amused gaze in the rearview mirror.

"The Roosevelt Hotel," he hollered.

The driver's face broke into a full fledged grin.

"No, wait," said Hunter. "Make it the apartment. I have to change."

If he was going to do this, he was going to do it right.

It was Sinclair's job to stay for the entire ball, not to mention the after party at the Castlebay Spa. While the orchestra played on, she looked longingly at her watch, then over to the exit. Maybe she could lay low in the lobby for a while. At least then she wouldn't have to dance with men she'd rather be talking promotions and P and L statements with.

What was it about a pretty dress and bit of makeup that turned men into babbling idiots? And why didn't Chantal care? Her life must be exhausting.

Mind made up, Sinclair headed for the lobby exit. At the very least, she deserved a break.

"Going somewhere, Sinclair?"

She whirled toward the familiar voice, sure her mind must be playing tricks.

He was dressed in a classic black tux, with a black bow tie and a matching cummerbund. His hair was perfect, his face freshly shaven, and his smile was the most wonderful thing she'd seen all day.

"I thought you'd be on the jet," she blurted out.

"I changed my mind."

"About going to London?"

"About a lot of things." He held out his arm. "Dance?"

Her spirit lifted, but her heart ached. Still, there was no way she'd turn him down.

"You look stunning, by the way," he mumbled as they moved toward the dance floor. "Zeppetti should pay you to wear his dresses."

"You're good for me," she said.

"No, you're good for me."

They attracted a small amount of attention as they moved through the crowd, probably more Hunter than her. People recognized him, and knew his position in the company.

When they reached the other dancers, he drew her into his arms. It felt like the most natural thing in the world, and she had to caution herself against reading anything into his actions. He was probably off to London tomorrow morning. When you had your own plane, you could do things like that. And Hunter enjoyed every facet of his freewheeling, billionaire lifestyle.

But, for now, she couldn't seem to stop herself from melting into his arms and pretending, just for a moment, that things could be different. They were still drawing glances from the other dancers. She could only hope her expression wouldn't make her the office gossip topic tomorrow.

Hunter drew her tight against his chest.

She wasn't sure, but she thought she felt a kiss on the top of her head.

Risky move in this crowd.

"You leaving after the ball?" she asked, hoping to keep some semblance of professionalism between them.

"Here's the thing," Hunter muttered, leaning very close to her ear. "I've gotten rather used to seeing you naked."

She coughed out a startled laugh. Then she tipped her head back to play along. "Why, you sweet talker."

He smiled down at her. "I've also gotten used to waking up with you wrapped in my arms."

Sinclair sobered. That was the part she thought she'd miss most—Hunter first thing in the morning, unshaven, unguarded, and always ready for romance.

"An office affair still isn't going to work," he went on.

She nodded and sighed. "I know." They'd talked about all the reasons why. And they were right about them.

"It would make us crazy to keep the secret. Plus, we'd eventually get caught."

Sinclair followed the steps as Hunter led her through the dance. He wasn't telling her anything she didn't already know.

"So, I was thinking," he said. "We should get married."

Sinclair stopped dead.

He leaned down. "Sinclair?"

She didn't answer. Was that her fevered imagination, or did he just…

"Better start dancing," he advised. "People are beginning to stare."

She forced her feet to move. "Did you just…"

"Propose?"

She nodded.

"Yes," he growled low. "I'm proposing that you and I get married, so we can spend every minute together, and nobody in the office will be able to say a damn thing about it."

Her brain still hadn't made sense of what he was saying. "Is this one of those reckless, impulsive things of yours?"

He shook his head. "Absolutely not. I've been considering this for at least an hour."

Despite the serious conversation, his tone made her chuckle.

"Okay, probably twenty-four hours," he said. "Ever since leaving you became a reality."

Sinclair blinked back tears of emotion.

"Or maybe it's been ten days, ever since I walked into that boardroom. Or," he paused. "Maybe since the first second I laid eyes on you." He wrapped her in a hug that didn't resemble any of the waltz moves she'd learned.

"It feels like I've loved you forever," he said.

"I love you, too." Her voice was muffled against his chest.

He drew back. "Is that a yes?"

"If you're sure."

"I am one-hundred-percent positive. I blew off the London deal for this."

"You're not going to London later?"

"Actually, I'm never leaving you again." He kissed her mouth, and she caught Roger's astonished expression as he danced by.

"Uh oh," she said.

"Well, we can separate occasionally. You know, during the day. But not overnight. I'm not—"

"Roger just saw you kiss me."

"Who cares?"

"He thinks I'm your floozy now."

"Don't worry about Roger. I caught him kissing Chantal behind the pillar when I walked in."

Sinclair was shocked. "Roger and Chantal?"

Hunter nodded.

It actually made sense. It explained a whole lot of things. But, strangely, Sinclair didn't care.

She shrugged.

Hunter sobered, looking deeply into her eyes. "You, me,

us, your job. You know none of it has anything to do with the other, right?"

Sinclair glanced at Roger a few dance couples away, straining his neck for a view of her and Hunter. "Roger doesn't."

In response Hunter kissed her again, longer this time.

Roger's eyes nearly popped out of his head.

"Wait till he gets a look at the rock on your finger."

"You have a rock?"

"Actually, no. I have nothing at the moment."

"Reckless and impulsive."

"Not at all. This is good planning." He took her hand in his, rubbing the knuckle of her ring finger. "We can glam this up as much as you want. But I was thinking something custom-made, to match you bracelet."

Sinclair held up her wrist. "I do seem to have developed a fondness for the fish."

Hunter fingered the delicate gold and jewels. "I always assumed I was the diamond one, and you were the ruby."

"I never thought about it," said Sinclair.

"Liar."

"Takes one to know one."

"Well, whatever we do, it better be fast."

"Good idea. Since that last kiss totally trashed my reputation with my coworkers."

Hunter glanced Roger's way. "He looks at you like that one more time, I'm making him president of the Osland button factory in Siberia."

"You don't have a button factory in Siberia."

"I'll buy one. It'll be worth it."

Sinclair's phone buzzed in her little purse.

"That'll be Kristy," said Hunter, nodding toward the faint sound.

"How do you know that?"

"Because she knows I'm here. I bet it's killed her to wait this long."

"You told her…"

"That I loved you? Yeah. I'll be telling everybody soon."

Sinclair snapped the clasp on her purse and retrieved the phone, putting it to her ear.

"Is he there?" Kristy stage-whispered.

"Who?" asked Sinclair innocently.

"You know who. What's going on? Tell me everything?"

"We're dancing."

"And?"

"And, I think we're getting married."

"You *know* we're getting married," Hunter called into the phone.

Kristy squealed so loud Sinclair had to pull it away from her ear.

"When? Where?" asked Kristy.

"Hunter seems to be in a hurry. Could you maybe give us the name of that place you and Jack used in Las Vegas?"

Hunter scooped the phone. "Negative on Vegas," he told Kristy. "I've reformed my impulsive ways. We're doing some methodical planning on this one." He glanced softly down at Sinclair. "I want it to be perfect."

Then he handed the phone back.

"I'm designing the dress," said Kristy.

"You bet you are," Sinclair agreed, watching the heat build in Hunter's eyes. "I better go now."

"Okay. But I'm flying out there as soon as possible."

"Just as long as you don't come tonight," said Sinclair, hanging up the phone over Kristy's laughter.

"Good tip," said Hunter.

"Excuse me, Sinclair," Roger interrupted, his mouth in a frown and a determined look in his eyes. "Can I speak with you—"

Hunter jumped in. "You might want to know—"

"This will only take a moment," said Roger.

"Really?" asked Hunter, brow going up.

Roger nodded.

Hunter anchored Sinclair to his side. "Sinclair has just accepted my marriage proposal."

Roger blinked in confusion, clearly the words were not computing.

"And I'd like to talk to you about a job opportunity for you," said Hunter. "My office? Tomorrow? Sometime in the afternoon."

Roger's brow furrowed. "I don't… You're getting *married?*"

Hunter nodded slowly.

Roger took a step back. "Oh…" Another step. "Well…" A third. "In that case…" He disappeared into the crowd.

"Funny that he didn't congratulate us," said Sinclair.

"He can send a card from Siberia." Hunter smoothly drew her into his arms and picked up the dance.

"Is Chantal going with him?"

"It would only be fair. Who am I to stand in the way of true love?"

"Who, indeed?" asked Sinclair, snuggling close to his broad chest. "And now you and I get to live happily ever after." She sighed.

"Just me, you and the twins."

"You believe the gypsy?"

Hunter nodded. "It has to be true. Jack's probably out there right now losing the family fortune. I just found out the

Castlebay Spa in Hawaii has a golf course. And with your red hair, twins would make it a clean sweep."

She laughed with joy over everything.

"I love you very much," Hunter whispered.

"And I love you," she whispered in return. "Happy Valentine's Day."

He hugged her tightly. "Happy Valentine's Day, sweetheart."

* * * * *

millsandboon.co.uk Community

Join Us!

The Community is the perfect place to meet and chat to kindred spirits who love books and reading as much as you do, but it's also the place to:

- **Get the inside scoop from authors about their latest books**
- **Learn how to write a romance book with advice from our editors**
- **Help us to continue publishing the best in women's fiction**
- **Share your thoughts on the books we publish**
- **Befriend other users**

Forums: Interact with each other as well as authors, editors and a whole host of other users worldwide.

Blogs: Every registered community member has their own blog to tell the world what they're up to and what's on their mind.

Book Challenge: We're aiming to read 5,000 books and have joined forces with The Reading Agency in our inaugural Book Challenge.

Profile Page: Showcase yourself and keep a record of your recent community activity.

Social Networking: We've added buttons at the end of every post to share via digg, Facebook, Google, Yahoo, technorati and de.licio.us.

www.millsandboon.co.uk

2 FREE BOOKS
AND A SURPRISE GIFT

We would like to take this opportunity to thank you for reading this Mills & Boon® book by offering you the chance to take TWO more specially selected books from the Modern™ series absolutely FREE! We're also making this offer to introduce you to the benefits of the Mills & Boon® Book Club™—

- **FREE home delivery**
- **FREE gifts and competitions**
- **FREE monthly Newsletter**
- **Exclusive Mills & Boon Book Club offers**
- **Books available before they're in the shops**

Accepting these FREE books and gift places you under no obligation to buy, you may cancel at any time, even after receiving your free books. Simply complete your details below and return the entire page to the address below. You don't even need a stamp!

YES Please send me 2 free Modern books and a surprise gift. I understand that unless you hear from me, I will receive 4 superb new books every month for just £3.19 each, postage and packing free. I am under no obligation to purchase any books and may cancel my subscription at any time. The free books and gift will be mine to keep in any case.

Ms/Mrs/Miss/Mr_____ Initials _____

Surname _____

Address _____

_____

_____ Postcode _____

Send this whole page to: Mills & Boon Book Club, Free Book Offer, FREEPOST NAT 10298, Richmond, TW9 1BR